With or Without

With or Without

and other stories

Charles Dickinson

Collier Books
Macmillan Publishing Company
New York

Macmillan Publishing Company
866 Third Avenue, New York, NY 10022
Collier Macmillan Canada, Inc.

"My Livelihood" first appeared in *Esquire*
"Risk" first appeared in *The Atlantic Monthly*
"Arcadia" first appeared in *Grand Street*
"Black Bart" first appeared in *Pikestaff Forum*
"Bill Boston," "Sofa Art," and "A Night in the Garden"
first appeared in *The New Yorker*
"1-800-YOUR BOY" first appeared in *The Atlantic Monthly*

Library of Congress Cataloging-in-Publication Data
Dickinson, Charles, 1951–
    With or without and other stories / Charles Dickinson.—1st
Collier Books ed.
        p.   cm.
    ISBN 0-02-019560-5
    I. Title.
PS3554.I324W5 1988
813'.54—dc19   87-31981
                                                              CIP

Cover illustration © by Joel Meyerowitz
Cover design by Lee Wade
First Collier Books Edition 1988

10 9 8 7 6 5 4 3 2 1

Printed in the United States of America

FOR SCOUT

ACKNOWLEDGMENTS

I have been fortunate to have worked with some of the finest editors in the business. For the expertise and insight they brought to these stories, my heartfelt thanks to Ricky Agent, James Atlas, Bob Gottlieb, Rust Hills, Alison Humes, Harrison McCormick, Dan Menaker, Ben Sonnenberg, Robert Sutherland, and Bruce Weber.

—CD

Contents

With or Without

My Livelihood

I lost my dairy job and was not troubled. One of my brothers-in-law said he could get me into the carpenters' union. He said he'd lend me the tools and instruct me in their use. I was tired of the dairy, all that whiteness every day, and the hairnets we had to wear. Hair in milk. Shows right up.

But I didn't want to be a carpenter, either. I wasn't looking for work. This bothered the hell out of my Stella, who was expecting our second child, hoping for a girl this time. She was six months gone. Two-thirds there, her belly was nice and round. Her cheeks were fat. My Stel is tall and took it well. She is very close to being pretty. My son's name is Ray.

My Stella's father is a contractor of some renown. He told me I was lazy. Her brothers, seven carpenters, said the same thing. Ray even picked it up: Daddy's lazy. Stella's family makes me nervous. They are too hearty in their work, out all day driving nails. They have muscles and great tans. They told me I could be a carpenter too and called me lazy when I said no thanks. I was waiting, I told myself. I felt something happening.

I'm thirty-three years old. I've been out of work a number of times in my life. Never like this, though, Stel tells me. She's right. I must avoid panic. I mustn't get roped into the first thing that pays. That is the old me. I was raised to hate work but to do it. I always had to have a job. This time I'm going slow.

The dairy told me *adios* April 15. My foreman called me into his office and said, "Kids ain't drinking the milk they used to." I didn't have the seniority to weather such a trend, but I liked the irony; Ray Boy drinks the stuff by the ton. Me and three other guys in hairnets went out the door. One guy started to cry and shake right there in the parking lot. A young guy, married, but no kids, he went right to pieces before my eyes. I shook hands all around, told the crying guy to grab hold. I got in my car and went straight home. Me for a sandwich and beer.

Along the way home I saw ads for things I couldn't afford anymore. On my dairy pay I couldn't afford most things, but there was always the chance; now, no way. The world was hung with ads, I noticed. All those deluxes beyond my reach.

I got out of my whites at home and threw them down the laundry chute. This was a small favorite with me, the boy in me coming out. I held on to the clothes until I could get my head in the chute to watch them fall; they got smaller falling, they stayed in flight longer than I expected. It was a cheap special effect and reminded me of science fiction.

Ray came home a little later and screamed when he saw me. I was out of place lying on the couch in the middle of the afternoon with a beer on my stomach. I gave him a hug. He said my arms smelled like cheese.

"Where's Mom?" I asked. He didn't know. I took him out back and we threw the Frisbee until Stella came home.

She brought an armload of old clothes with her. More Goodwill crap. Her face glowed with the pleasure of doing good for others. She dropped a black shoe when she came to the door to call Ray and saw me running after the flying saucer.

"Why are you home?" she asked.

"I lost my job."

My Stella wet her lips with her tongue. She carried the old

clothes into the utility room and dropped them on the floor. I picked up the black shoe and followed her. She gave me a kiss. Wet salt taste. Her stomach bumping me. I felt a rising. When was the last time we'd done it in the afternoon? I was always working. Ray Boy. Something. See, I told myself, a positive thing already.

"It's not so bad," I told her. "Nothing to worry about."

I looked outside at Ray. He was talking to a kid on a bike and throwing the Frisbee up and catching it. I suggested to my Stella, "Let's go upstairs."

She stepped behind the pile of clothes. She wanted that crap between us, I guess. Her face had changed. I felt the moment getting away from me. My Stel wanted me to be afraid for our quality of life. She'd kissed me, sure, but she'd also bumped me with her hard belly. Number two, hello in there.

"Nothing to be worried about?" she said. She was tapping one of her feet, which are big.

"It'll be all right," I said.

She was not ready for this. My Stella is the baby of her family, though she is older than two of her brothers. Stella and her mother and father and seven brothers. Her father paid for our house as a wedding present. Her brothers built it. I remember that as a hard time for me. Her brothers had something to do, they laughed at each other's jokes. I just sat on the lumber and watched. I fetched them beers to make myself useful.

Stella had been raised in a world that was a happy place. All lines were plumb, all nails were straight. Her grandfather was dead a year, flattened by a slipped ton of bricks, before Stel was told. She was not prepared for a husband out of work. I saw her start to cry. Her mother's tears. It was the lone soft spot in the men in Stella's family, and that spot was mush. Don't use it too often, I could hear Stella's mother coaching her, dry-eyed. Use it sparingly and it will hit home every time.

I took a step forward, kissed my wife, and smiled. I would not be bullied. If she kept it up, I'd go outside and play with Ray.

"Pretty soon . . . pretty soon," my Stella sobbed, bringing one of her big feet up through the pile of Goodwill crap, filling the air with it, "we'll be wearing this stuff ourselves."

I got into a poker game with some of the dairy guys, and though I won $122 I went home sad. All that dairy talk, it made me miss it. Tales of women on the routes. Stray things that dropped in the milk. A driver named Del was being sued for running over a champion Afghan. He laughed and said the dog looked like an old flame, and that was why he went after it, but still he was being sued. They let me play but I didn't belong. I imagined they were mad because I was ungrateful enough to win, too.

My Stella saw me sitting at home and decided I was sad and bored. She dragged me along on her Goodwill rounds. "It will do you good to get out of the house," she said. "It will lift your spirits until you find another job."

"My spirits aren't low."

"Yes they are," she told me.

At every place we stopped she worked the fact of my unemployment into the conversation. I'd stand out by the car and she'd point at me, and I'd wave and smile. She might have asked for something in my size. She used me as an example of the type of person all those rags would help.

When I asked her not to tell everybody I'd lost my job, she answered with words that even made a little sense. "These people are very successful, and you never know who might offer you a job."

We stopped at the Blatt house. Mrs. Blatt was going to donate an old set of golf clubs to Goodwill. I offered to buy them from her for ten dollars.

"You'll do no such thing," my Stella protested.

"Here." I folded the bill in Mrs. Blatt's hand. I saw it in her eyes: charity was fine, but profit was holy. "You can get rid of the clubs," I told her, "and make a little money."

I slung that bag of jangling sticks over my shoulder. "People who need Goodwill don't have time to play golf," I told Stella. "They're too busy looking for firewood."

I took my clubs to the public course the next day. The new ball I teed up reminded me guiltily of an egg that should have been on Ray Boy's plate, and that reminded me of my joblessness. But then I hit the ball and it swooped out of sight. The feeling was solid in my hands. A motion down the fairway caught my eye. My ball landing. It hit and rolled, it might have gone forever but the ground was damp. I set off after it. I played thirty-six holes that day.

I never was an athlete. My father owned a grocery and I went to work for him when I was seven years old, cheap help, a roof over my head and a dollar allowance a week making me, in my father's words, "rich enough." I worked in that store for an hour before school, then after school until we closed at seven, and all day on weekends. I was ringing sales on the cash register when I was nine years old and all the kids my age were outdoors hitting baseballs or shooting free throws. These kids came indoors in winter, red-faced, to buy gum or oatmeal cookies, skates hanging from their necks. Their taped sticks and black disks were exotic tools to me. I was a flop in gym. I once brained myself getting under a fly ball and probably survived only because we were playing softball.

One day, I was fifteen, I stopped to watch the golfers on my way to work. For more than two years they had been building the course, and all that land hadn't meant much to me. I had seen the yellow graders and the scalloped dents filled with sand and the troops of Mexicans brought in to lay rolls of sod. It had meant nothing to me. I clerked in a grocery for my old man.

Then the golf course opened. I was passing by and saw a guy on the tee, and I watched him whip his club around and smack that ball a mile, though I couldn't see where it landed.

The guy watched it and watched it, then slid his club into a bag and covered it with a tasseled sock.

This was golf. It looked like something I might like. There were no moving balls to hit or control. I would not be required to be quick, or to do something instantly for the good of the team. But I didn't dare tell my father. I had a job; that was all I needed. Eighteen years would pass before I would tee it up.

I have two brothers, three sisters. I think that's part of why I fell in love with Stella; she understood the big-family life. All of us worked in the store. My mother, too. When my sister Diana got up the money and nerve to leave and was planning to move to Phoenix, my old man snuck into her room the night before she was to leave and cut up her bus ticket. Diana avenged this by upending every pyramid of cans in the store at the height of the Saturday rush. A terrific racket. We watched and cheered and refused to restack them. We never came closer to open revolt.

Why did we stay and work there so long? It was part of our training. All of us realize that now. My father hated that store. He told us so often how he hated it that we hated it, too. Now none of us can stand the things we do for a living. To the old man, work was a curse. Now it is to us, too. We may like the money, or maybe the people on the job, or the end of the day, but none of us gets anything from the actual work. It makes me angry. My father had no right. This is one reason I'm not looking right now.

Diana finally got to Phoenix and became a cocktail waitress and hooker. I've seen pictures of her taken there. She's a pretty girl, though I don't recognize her as my sister. She says she hates her jobs. Rachel is a nurse and hates it. She writes me long letters from Boston, filled with complaint. She hates the old man's ghost for what he gave her. That ghost has driven us all away. Me here, Rachel in Boston, Diana in Arizona, Tim in Paris, of all places, Rosie in Vancouver. Vic owns a bait-and-tackle shop in the Upper Peninsula of Michigan, on the shore of Lake Superior, and hires kids to run it for him. He told me they rob him blind, but he accepts this as the price he has to pay to be able to stay away from the place.

My father died when I was twenty-one. My mother sold the store and split the proceeds evenly among herself and her children. It made a nice lump, and it is this, to some extent, that feeds my family now. Vic bought the bait shop with his share. Rachel put hers into nursing-school tuition.

My mother took her share and moved to New Orleans. I visited her once and she made me cry, she was so content. She lived in a large apartment that had a thousand plants, French doors, and a thin strip of balcony you could stand on and smell the Gulf of Mexico. She cooked a ton of shrimp for us. She played Bingo every night. She sat in that smoky room and inhaled deeply. She was good. She claimed to have increased her inheritance by a fourth. I liked that she had her groceries delivered by lanky black boys eager for the good tip she was known for. She's still there.

So my father's death and the store's being sold was my first taste of being out of work. I stashed my inheritance and panicked. I took the first job I could find, going to work in a factory that made gizmos for detecting police radar. I sat on a high stool under perfect light doing the same four steps over and over again. It was boring work and I kind of liked it the first three hours. But the business was on the rise, and automation came along and did my job better. Last hired, I was first fired. That was only fair. A second time I was out of work.

I knocked around a few years. I worked odd jobs and tested my reactions to losing them. It was like giving myself increasing jolts of electricity to see how much I could stand. The longest I went without work, without looking for work, was three weeks. I started waking up depressed, bathed in sweat. I knew I had to find work right away. It was not lack of money that drove me, but something deeper. It was the values of my father, what he had nailed in me with all those hours in the store. Hating work was in my blood.

I'm a glib guy when I have to be. Getting a job has never been a problem. I come across as earnest, reliable, eager to do the job. I knew that once I started looking I'd find something right away. When I was twenty-five, I took a job working for the city at a recycling center, real moron's work that paid $7.70 an hour, a king's ransom. My job was to sort all the crap people brought in to have recycled, weigh the stuff, and throw it in the respective dumpsters to be hauled away. We took in only glass bottles, aluminum cans, and newspapers.

We paid twenty cents a pound for aluminum cans. A tall young lady with a kind of obsessed look on her face argued with me one day that our scales were off, that I was cheating her. I explained that the scales were accurate, that she'd have to trust me, but that if she wanted to complain, she could go up to the village hall and talk to them. She said she just might. I weighed her cans and wrote out her receipt. I watched her walk to her car, an emerald Lincoln Continental, and maneuver her body into it. She had large hips, breasts, and feet and was almost six feet tall. She didn't seem comfortable with all she had been given. It looked like too much for her to handle. I guessed she was twenty or twenty-one and would learn to be graceful later. Of course, this girl was my Stella.

She was back in a week with more cans, bags of them stuffed in the trunk and back seat of her Lincoln. I asked where she got them all.

"Along the highway," she said. "Everywhere you look. People can be such pigs."

I asked if that was how she paid for her car, smiling to let her know I was flirting.

"My daddy bought my car for me."

She kept returning with cans all that summer, and when I

drove home I always was surprised to see any cans along the road, I was sure she had gotten them all. She had an anxious face. She was eager for something, and late in July I began to have dreams that it was me. I asked her for a date the next time she was in. She agreed and volunteered to drive. We went miniature-golfing and had a pizza on our first date. On other dates we necked in her wide back seat. She was clumsy with her size only until she got in my arms. Then her grace and invention were startling. She began driving me to and from work; on occasion, we scouted the highway together for cans, though I lacked her prospector's lust. The first time I took her clothes off I was amazed at all that was involved. My Stella, big, smooth-skinned riddle. We were married in a year. Ray Boy soon followed. I was making $10.11 an hour at the recycling center and hating it so much it had the feel of a career. Then about a year ago my Stella came home and told me her father knew someone at the dairy, that he could get me a job if I was interested.

I played 180 holes the first week of May. My Goodwill clubs were in sorry condition but I didn't mind. After I scraped the crud from their faces they worked fine. When I wasn't on the course, I was practicing in my yard with plastic golf balls.

The pro at the public course where I played told me my swing was "a natural" and that it could really be spruced up with a few lessons. I had no use for lessons. If I was taking a lesson, that would mean less time I'd be out on the course actually playing. I was afraid to take golf seriously. I was afraid I'd learn to hate the game.

The pro told me I was lazy. "You have to put some effort into it," he told me.

"Effort," I said, "implies resistance."

I hit the ball long and straight from the first. I didn't lust after scores like so many guys who were out to break a hundred, then ninety, then eighty. I was living on that fascination for the game planted eighteen years earlier when I'd seen that guy hitting his drive on my way to work. I was playing. It was a strange thing: work and play. Some days, if I was short or didn't feel like spending my money on a round, I worked it off in the pro shop washing balls, cleaning clubs, or filling driving-range buckets for Dave, who ran the place. When I did finally get out on the course, I wasn't ashamed of my clubs or my shoes (which I paid two dollars for at a garage sale; they fit perfectly but one was missing a heel cleat). I had a sport. And when my playing partners had to quit to go back to work, I could play all afternoon.

June came. The summer was dry and hot. I could feel the greens quickening by the moment. My Stella's face got fatter. I was in the front yard practicing my nine iron when one of my brothers-in-law appeared. This one was named Jack. He was about forty years old, with thick forearms, a tan, and a cigarillo in his mouth.

"How's she holding up?" he asked.

"Just fine."

"No leaks?"

"Stella?"

Jack broke off a laugh and walked up to the house he had helped build. He smacked the wall. "No, man! Our house. A damn fine job we did for you."

"The house is fine," I assured him. I had seven plastic balls lined up at my feet. One by one I would hit them down the yard. I looked forward to Jack leaving so I could get on with it.

"Stel tells us you're still out of work."

"Stel tells everybody that," I said. "I expect to see it on the news."

"Been a while, hasn't it?"

I swung smoothly through the first ball and it floated away with a faint *snick!* sound. I liked Jack best of that hopeless knot of carpenters I had married into. He was the oldest, and the only one to thank me for the beers I fetched while they built our house. Not much of a swap, I know, beers for a house, but I appreciate good manners wherever they occur.

"We'll be OK," I said. "Thanks for your concern."

"You got any prospects?"

"Prospects for a job? I haven't been looking too hard."

"You've got a pregnant wife in there, pal," Jack said.

"No. She's not home."

He grimaced. Me, the smart ass. "What do you do with yourself all day?"

"I play a lot of golf. You play?"

"No. Look, how about being a carpenter? We can get you in the union."

"No, thanks."

"Dad said he can call in a few favors. It's good money. The work is seasonal, sure, but when you work, the money is damn good."

"I can't even hammer a nail, Jack." With the softest *tick!* I sent the next ball away down a sweet, high path.

Jack dismissed my ineptitude. "That can be taught. Any asshole can drive a nail. We'll lend you some tools until you can get your own. With a little pull from Dad we can even skip your apprenticeship. You'll start right off in the serious money."

"You've given us enough already," I told him. I settled myself over the next ball. Jack momentarily ceased to be. I hit it nicely. "This house," I said, "and I know your father gives Stella money. I can't take another job from you, too."

"Is that so terrible? Taking something from your family during hard times?"

"Yeah, Jack. It's gotten to that point."

"It's not easy getting into the union. The waiting list is a mile long."

"Let someone in who wants to be a carpenter."

"It's true, I guess, what Stel says."

"Probably," I agreed.

"She says you're lazy. She says you like being out of a job."

"My Stella speaks the truth."

My Stella gave us a daughter on a steamy August morning. Cecilia Joan was a big girl like her mother, coming in an ounce shy of ten pounds. I laid my hand on Stella's wet forehead and put my ear to her chest to listen to her heart. She had worked hard. The baby was red and creased. We took our mothers' first names, flipping a coin to determine the order.

The elevator dumped a load of carpenters. We heard them coming and Stella laughed. She rolled her tired eyes at me and hooked her lank hair behind her ears. She knew I'd be leaving soon.

Her father led them in. He carried a giant stuffed panda.

"So here's the numbnuts who's too good to be a carpenter," he said. "Too good to be helped out by his family that works up a sweat on the job."

"Daddy!" Stella protested.

They filled the room with the smell of pine. Shavings hung in their hair. Their pants were functionally adorned with loops and slots to hold the gizmos of their calling. They had brought fragile nightery and bluebird mobiles.

"Mr. Out-of-Work don't know what a sweet deal he blew," Stella's father pressed.

I kissed my pretty wife goodbye. Her forehead tasted of salt. Already her face looked not so fat.

"See you, boys," I said to the carpenters, and made my way through them to the door.

I met three strangers and we went out. I played my round to an eighty-nine. The others finished in the high nineties and low one hundreds. These men were quick to anger; they beat themselves. I counted a half-dozen times when each of them could have made a run at me, but I knew they wouldn't. Over the summer I'd learned to read my opponents by the hunch of their shoulders or the smoke from their ears, and to know when another bad shot was about to emerge to compound their anguish. I waited for these moments and threw a bet their way just before they shot. They would straighten up, glare at me, and accept. They hated themselves for being less than perfect; now they had bet on it. A vein of cash ran from their brains to my wallet.

Toward the end of the day, I waited in the pro shop drinking lemonade.

"Didn't do much today," observed Dave.

"Too hot," I agreed.

"Too hot for anything."

"Hey, Dave! I'm a father!"

Dave smiled at me. "No shit?"

"Second time around," I said. "But undeniably no shit."

"That's great." He shook my hand. "You got any cigars?"

I patted my pockets. "Sorry."

"That's a screwy tradition anyhow," Dave said. "The father'll be paying out the nose all his life. He should be the one getting the see-gars."

"Amen," I said.

"So what can I give you, Dad?"

"New set of sticks?"

"Be serious, Dad."

"A free round?"

"Play on, Dad."

I found a foursome. We moved over the course through a cooling dusk. Bugs swirled in the pro shop's lights. I was pushing up the fairway on my thirty-sixth hole of the day. I planned to shower, have a beer, then get Ray Boy and go visit his mother and sister. I felt pretty grand. I was on in three. Nobody could stop me from winning money on the round. And nobody said I couldn't win a little more.

My opponents had been at work and had come to catch the late-afternoon reduced fees. They played the front nine as though still in suits and ties. They bitched about their work between shots. They expected too much. Their anger increased and I skimmed it like cream.

On the eighteenth green I turned to one of them, a guy named Herb. He could not believe he trailed me by seven strokes. He was on in three, too.

"Ten to whoever gets down from here first?" I said.

"Yeah." He jumped at the chance.

I let him go first because I liked to savor any day's last putts. They always made me a little sad. What promise did I have I'd ever play again? Away from the game I was just another guy out of work.

Herb jerked his first putt eight feet past the cup. I easily rolled mine within a foot. I tapped in to get out of his way. No problem, he went wide. I swear his eyes were glowing.

They paid me my due in the twilight. Herb had to write me a check (he kept his checkbook in his bag, as though he suspected something about himself), and I accepted it gracefully. Another guy paid me in quarters.

All this money amazed me; my livelihood was seasonal, like carpentry.

A coin fell through my fingers while I was putting my earnings in my wallet. I left it there on the green for a fellow player to mark his ball.

Bill Boston

Here is Bill Boston, long rumored dead, advancing with a beautiful woman up the wide avenue. Hooper sees him coming and, awkward with disbelief, turns toward a window full of ladies' shoes and handbags. In the mirror of the glass, Hooper watches Bill Boston and the woman pass behind him. Bill is laughing, and the woman looks warmed and delighted by her talent for making him laugh. They are holding hands.

Hooper follows. The woman has long legs. She is wearing flat sandals, and her bare toenails are painted coral. A burgundy silk skirt dances around her like a loose circle of worshippers. Her hair is a soft gold cut one length. Her squared shoulders shake when she laughs.

But Hooper studies Bill Boston more intently. His thick body is less the wedge of muscle Hooper remembers. The neck is thinner, sunburned, and finely creased. The heavy chest that used to drive straight through tacklers is succumbing a little to gravity, and the waist is pushing out. But he walks with the jauntiness Hooper remembers. The sleeves of his pinstriped shirt are rolled up, and he carries his suit coat hooked on a finger over his shoulder. And Bill's hair has not changed—so blond as to be white. He still wears it shaped tight on a stony skull. When he played football in high school, he told Hooper he wanted to feel the game through his head—the pinch of his helmet, the blows taken and imparted. Hooper follows the handsome couple, hanging a half-block behind, his hands curled around coins and car keys in his pockets, too stunned and shy and embarrassed to approach.

It was in a letter from his mother that Hooper got the first word of trouble in Bill Boston's life. Tucked like a sliver of glass among the gossip and idle information was the news that Bill was very sick. That was eight years ago, not long after Bill and his family moved away. In her next letter, she wrote, "Billy had cancer and underwent surgery that was not entirely successful. He lost his beautiful hair. He saw what he had become, so he decided to take his life. That is what I've heard."

Hooper had a hard time believing it. "Mother," he wrote back, "that's a strong story for having no concrete basis in fact, as far as you know."

"I believe it," his mother replied. She said that the news had come from a woman whose daughter once loved Bill Boston, long ago. She was a girl Hooper's mother wished had loved Hooper instead. This girl was now married, the mother of two beautiful little girls, and, Hooper's mother reported, "she cried like a baby when she heard about Billy, or so her mother said."

Hooper answered, "That is a convincing detail," and since he could neither confirm nor deny the report—since he had no contrasting evidence firmer than strong memories of his friend —as far as he knew, Bill Boston had killed himself.

Clarinet music in summer would slide across the lawn from Bill Boston's room into Hooper's room. In winter Hooper saw into Bill's room, saw him with his lips on the reed, his big hands moving deftly over the long tube of black, with its stops and valves like configurations of frozen silver. Hooper strained to hear. The music bumped up against the cold windows of Bill Boston's room, packing the room tight, until finally Hooper would grow frustrated and telephone. "Play *Rhapsody in Blue*," he would request.

"It's your dime," Bill Boston would say, and would set the phone down and play into it—a singular broadcast.

Bill Boston had an unfortunate first step, his coaches said; it kept him out of a Big Ten backfield. But he had drive and never fumbled. He held the football with as much care as his clarinet, enfolding it like a child, transporting it. By his third step he was going full bore. Hooper watched in envy and awe at the opponents hitting and caroming off Bill Boston's advancing form. And at that point of inevitability, when the odds were too lopsided and opposing players hung from him like huge, bruised fruit and he was going to be tackled, Bill Boston dropped his stone head like a ram and skewered to the ground any poor guy in his path.

One day he told Hooper, "I'm going to Brown."

"Will you play?"

"Yes, they want me. I can play football. Be in the band. Be a student."

Hooper had nothing to say. His own life lacked the momentum of Bill Boston's. He would get out of high school with nothing waiting for him. He had no idea what he was going to do.

"I once thought I could play in the NFL," Bill said, "but I don't want to fool myself anymore. I could probably hang on at some football factory, but what's the point? I couldn't be in the band. I wouldn't play regularly. I'm not quick. I'm steady and I have heart. But I tapped the last of my talent this year. I won't get any better. Time to move on."

He went to Brown, and on Sunday mornings Hooper would see lines of small type in the back of the sports pages devoted to East Coast football results, and, frequently, to Brown and to Bill Boston, local boy. In his very first varsity game he rushed for ninety-one yards and two touchdowns in a 37–28 loss to Colgate. Then no word for several weeks, until Bill Boston ran for eighty-seven yards and a touchdown in a 10–0 win over Bucknell.

He came home for Christmas with a small mouse under his left eye. His grades arrived after the New Year—five A's.

"I'm in love, Hoop," Bill said. They drank beer in a little club in town where jazz was played.

"She's older than me," he said. "Her name is Susan Lock-erman. She's gorgeous. She's in med school. She plays the piano. I met her when she worked off and on as our trainer."

Hooper had nothing to counter with: no love, no passion, no good news, nothing he cared about. "She talked me into going into medicine," Bill said. "It's what I'm going to do, Hoop. It's what I wanted to do all along, I believe, and never knew it. She was placed in my path to meet and fall in love with and show me what to do."

Hooper said nothing. He looked beyond Bill Boston into the smoky pockets of the club, at all the people who would be there the next time he was in; Bill Boston was passing through on his way to better things. Maybe Bill understood this, too— that he had moved beyond this part of the world. He didn't say much the rest of the evening, and they said a brief good-night on the sidewalk outside their houses. It was the last time Hooper saw Bill Boston until he appeared on the street with the beautiful woman.

Bulletins of success reached Hooper from the newspaper and from his mother. Bill Boston rushed for 1,017 yards and fourteen touchdowns his senior season at Brown. The Colts drafted him in the eleventh round, but he declined to attend their camp, instead enrolling in Stanford medical school and marrying Dr. Susan Lockerman.

Later came word of Bill Boston's illness. Later still, word of his suicide. Hooper did not have the courage or the energy to seek out the truth. He was contented. He lived a life of diminished resistance. No heartaches. He had a wife, a son, a job selling business forms. He met his father one night a week to play cribbage and drink beer.

His parents had split up earlier. His mother surprised him by being the one to leave town. Her letters came sketched on florid sheets of stiff paper posted with gay, lively-colored stamps. His father refused to read the letters but always asked how his mother was.

One night, Hooper told his father, "She says Bill Boston is dead."

"That's a damn shame."

"I wonder if it can be true."

"You don't just make up a story like that," his father said.

"No. You wouldn't think so." But Hooper still had a hard time believing it.

Life rounded out for Hooper. Sometime in his thirties a conviction seized him that put a small spark in his heart. He had grown to love his work. Three years in a row he was his firm's top salesman. The small gold spindle presented to each year's top salesman became known as a Hooper. This fact marked his life with a kind of immortality. He would live on. He mourned Bill Boston's rumored passing at that moment; he had no one from his past to tell.

On a sales trip to Chicago he ran into the woman who as a girl had loved Bill Boston—the woman who had supposedly been the original source of the news of Bill Boston's death. She greeted Hooper with the same diffidence she had shown him in high school. They talked to each other for a good five minutes—dancing in their tracks, for it was a cutting winter wind they stood in—without mention of Bill Boston. Hooper longed to ask this woman whether she knew for certain that Bill Boston was dead, but after they waved and walked on he imagined she didn't know, and held the same desire to know shielded behind her heart, like a last match. Then he supposed that she knew the truth and did not need to ask him, and Bill Boston's death struck him again.

That year, he won his fourth Hooper in five years. His boss, at the awards banquet, claimed to have calculated that if all the receipts and stationery and bills of lading and inventory forms Hooper had sold in his eleven years with the company were stacked atop each other they would rise 311 miles into the sky and be visible three states away. Hooper laughed along with everybody else, but he was thinking of Bill Boston—that he was not alive to know about the bit of greatness Hooper was achieving at last.

The eve of their first day in high school, a fragrant mild night filled with fireflies like brief comets, Hooper and Bill Boston sat on the grass between their houses.

"Hoops," Bill said, "what are you going to get your letter in?"

Hooper had no idea. He could throw a Frisbee and catch it, but beyond that he was lost. Bill Boston already had his wedged physique and careful hands; he was a young football phenom coveted by the high-school coaches. A coach from a Catholic school had approached Bill with an invitation to attend there—the studies were solid, they routinely sent players to Notre Dame's fabled fields. Bill Boston had politely declined.

"I know I'll letter in football," Bill Boston said easily that last summer night. He did, and he also played the clarinet. He was first chair by his junior year. Hooper never won a letter. The time closed up behind him, wasted. He was lost all four years. Away from school the time was clearer: he was shut up gratefully in his small room while his mother and father chewed at each other downstairs. Around and around. He would phone Bill Boston to play something for him: "Mack the Knife," "Smoke Gets in Your Eyes," "Moon Over Miami," "My Blue Heaven," "Stranger on the Shore."

Finally Bill Boston would say, "I've got to study."

"OK. Thanks."

"Your mom and dad really go at it."

"Yeah. Sorry you have to listen to it."

"Don't worry about me. But, Jesus, they just beat the same dead horses every night."

"Tell me about it," Hooper said. "Thanks for the music," he added, and hung up.

No letter. No music. The same dead horses. Now he and his father are fair friends. His father is retired and seems to regret those long nights of combat with Hooper's mother. She is gone. They are both alone, and what for? He asks his son this in a roundabout fashion. What was the point of all that bile?

"The fires that woman lit in my gut have all died down," he told Hooper—a vision with a poetic light, Hooper thought. "I miss the old battle-ax, I really do."

"Sure, Dad," Hooper said. His mother was wise and safe hundreds of miles away.

Hooper, because of the fights that echoed in his memory, was kind and solicitous toward his wife. She even claimed he was too nice, too mild. But though there were times she enraged him, he kept a memory of his parents' wars close and maintained a good nature.

She accused him of a lack of passion. She wanted their emotions to run to extremes. He could not see the point, and told her of Bill Boston, who worked feverishly at everything, even love, and was dead now.

"Bill Boston! Bill Boston!" his wife shouted. "For someone dead, he sure gets around."

"What do you mean?"

"I mean he's everywhere. I turn around and there he is again. You must bring him up three times a day."

"I don't," Hooper said, with a cautious smile. Did he truly invoke Bill Boston so frequently?

"Just about," she said.

"I hardly knew him at all after high school," he said.

Hooper has lost Bill Boston and the woman in the lunchtime crowds. He looks for that characteristic white hair but does not see it. He stops and lights a cigar, then turns and resumes his day. He notes the avenue, though, and the hour, and the following day he is back waiting on one of the concrete-and-cedar benches the city has erected up and down the avenue to lure people to tarry in the dying downtown. The benches are popular in the sunlight. A pair of old men sit and argue to Hooper's left, while to his right a young woman goes through her parcels in search of something. But Hooper can't imagine anyone except street gangs and thieves using the benches at night—to catch their breath between crimes. The word "POPES" has been painted in orange letters a foot tall on the sidewalk, like a concise recruiting poster. No place to be after dark, this.

Four straight days he sits and smokes, waiting for Bill Boston. Then comes the weekend, and on Monday he is kept away on business. He is certain that this is the time Bill Boston and the woman will make their graceful passage up the avenue.

He wonders what he would say to Bill Boston if he saw him again. He could tell him about his four Hoopers. He could tell him about his wife and son. He could tell Bill Boston he is glad to see him alive—there was this crazy rumor. And beyond that? Ask him about his life in medicine. Ask him about his clarinet. Maybe sell him some stationery. Memo pads: "From the desk of Bill Boston." Ask him about the beautiful woman. Where does she fit in?

"Guess who I thought I saw on the street last week," Hooper says to his wife that Monday night.

She is spooning peas into a bowl. She says, "Bill Boston."

"Yeah! How'd you guess?"

"You've been talking in your sleep."

"I have?"

"You've been keeping me awake," she says. "Long monologues about Bill Boston, this wonder man with white hair, ex–football star, clarinet player, physician, ladies' man. Suicide." She clangs the lid on the pan. "He sounds boring to me," she says.

"Oh, no. You'd love him."

"I doubt it." She goes to the door and calls to their son.

"But I saw him on the street," Hooper says. "There was some doubt . . . I was never absolutely positive he died. It was really never more than a rumor."

"Maybe he's alive, then." She sips her iced tea; she cleans her glasses with the tail of her shirt. One of his Hoopers is on the kitchen counter, with recipes and notes spiked on the thin gold needle.

Their son comes through the door smiling. He sweeps through them like a wind as he goes to wash for dinner. Hooper has watched his son for a sign of musical talent or intellectual genius or a consuming passion, and has found none. He takes after his dad. He is just a ten-year-old kid with nothing particular on his mind. When he returns to the table, Hooper sees that he has missed a grass stain on his cheek. His mother wets her finger and with tender impatience rubs the stain away.

"He could go through a car wash and miss a spot," Hooper says.

His son aims a careful look at him. He sees his father means no harm, and smiles. He is moving into that long, painful time, Hooper thinks, when Dad becomes something looming and dangerous in a young man's life. Hooper remembers no clear details of that time of his own life—only the racket of battle downstairs—but understands fully its power and significance. A hard time for son and father. The kid begins to understand the father, and nothing is ever the same again. What's a boy to believe in after that?

Bill Boston's father—Hooper remembers while his family eats; he feels he is sneaking away from them—was a soft-spoken man who always seemed to be working in the yard or around the house. He was possessed of some inner agitation, for at odd moments his face would squeeze out of shape as though tightening itself against a great pain.

"He won't tell us what it is," Bill Boston said once. "My mom and I bug him about it, but it doesn't exist for him except for those few moments when his face falls apart."

So when he meets Bill Boston on the street he can also ask, "How's your father?"

He has added this to the list he carries in his head when he takes a seat on the bench the next day. It is almost noon, and the wide avenue is filled with people, automobiles, buses, smoking trucks, taxis. There is noise and dirt and the fine black residue he must wash from his hair every night, but the faces of the people are happy to be alive and moving in the world.

Hooper lights a cigar and crosses his legs. That morning he sold a computer company in Austin, Texas, eighty-seven thousand dollars' worth of letterhead stationery and bills of lading. He will win another Hooper if the other salesmen are not careful. He will put ground between himself and the rest of the field until he is just a receding speck on the—

Here is Bill Boston coming up the avenue, holding the hand of the beautiful woman, his coat hooked on his finger over his shoulder. That white hair, those careful hands. A pager hangs from his belt. He could be summoned at a moment's notice to rush off to save a life.

Hooper stands up and moves behind them, just off Bill Boston's right shoulder. He says, "Billy."

The man and the woman stop and turn to look at Hooper,

his voice is so near and so certain. But Hooper sees that this is not Bill Boston. Close, but no. The same white hair. The thick build. But this stranger, looking back with a question in his eyes, lets his suit coat fall from his finger to the sidewalk, and that isn't something Bill Boston would allow.

Risk

Owen is the host tonight. Washing glasses, he flips them in the air until they are just winks in the light. Catching them again takes his breath away.

Frank is the first to arrive. Then Nolan. Frank wore dirty clothes that afternoon when he took his laundry down to the big machines in the basement of his apartment building; with the load in the washer, soap measured, and coins slotted, he added the clothes he was wearing and made the long walk back upstairs to his apartment naked. He paused to read the fine print on the fire extinguisher. Noises in the building set birds loose in his heart. Frank takes the red armies when they gather to play the game of world conquest.

They hear Alice arrive in a storm of gravel. She has moved herself stoned across twenty-two miles of back roads in just under twenty minutes. She lives with a man she has know for seven months, in a rented farmhouse on a hundred acres of land. The man is good with a garden and with his hands, a warmhearted, full-bearded man who plays the banjo professionally, an amicable host when the game is at their house. He loves Alice, but still she meets another man on the sly. Half her appointments and reasons for being away from home are fabrications. This other man treats her like a child, making fun of the gaps in her knowledge, hurting her feelings, which she perversely enjoys. It is a counterpoint to the sweet man at home. Alice plays black.

The world is arranged on Owen's kitchen table. A strong yellow light shines down through the night's first gauzy sheets of smoke. The game's six continents—North and South America, Africa, Asia, Europe, and Australia—are not entirely faithful to the earth's geography. Each continent is formed from territories, and between these territories war will soon be waged with armies and dice.

Owen pours Frank a beer. Owen hosts as often as possible; he would play three or four times a week if he could. The gathering of his friends soothes him and fills dark spaces in the house. The smoke softens edges. He tries to get Eileen, his wife, to play, but she refuses. She remains in the other rooms. None of the players press on this point of awkwardness.

Owen shuffles through the game cards, a glass of beer at his elbow, a cigarette in an ashtray. Alice comes into the kitchen and shades her glassy eyes. "Hi," she says.

"Speak for yourself," Frank says.

Nolan, who has arrived in a sour mood, says, "The nation's motorists are safe for a few hours."

Alice hangs her coat on the tree by the door. She takes her makings out of her purse and carefully arranges them by her place at the board.

"Wine in the fridge," Owen says. "I'll get it for you in a second." He shakes the white dice and throws them across the face of the world. A pair of fives and a six.

"Oo," Alice says. "Hot."

"I'll take that all night."

Frank asks, "Who's late again?"

Les is late again; he makes a point of it. He never offers to host, nor does he ever bring beer or food. He feels that his presence is sufficient. Les always rolls good dice. It is something he demands of himself. He wins more often than the other players. From early March to early December, he drives a 1,000cc motorcycle without a helmet. The others allow him to continue to play despite his cheap habits because he is so good; to bar him would be cowardly. But Frank has dreamed of Les hitting ice on his cycle, his unprotected head bouncing sweetly on the highway.

Les and Pam arrive at the same time, though not together. Les's hair is swept back like Mercury's wings. Where Les is allowed to play because he is the best player, Pam, the worst, is invited back because she is so generous and so good-looking. She has large green eyes, long curly pale-red hair, and heavy breasts tucked into a loose sweater. She is usually the last to arrive and the first to lose all her armies and be eliminated. She has been playing for a year and still does not have a handle on the game. She tries to have a sense of humor about this. She always brings a large bag of pretzels and two six-packs of Dutch beer. She is always welcome. She plays pink.

Pam is in love with Nolan. She tries to catch his eye from across the room as she hands Owen her sack of food and beer. She has been with Nolan just that afternoon. It is stitched in her memory in dim light. The run through stinging branches to his basement, their time there, their almost being caught by his wife. They met at one of these gatherings and have known each other a year; Nolan's presence kept her coming back after she learned that she was not very good at the game and probably never would be. She liked his lean frame and dark-blue eyes and the clever look his glasses gave him. But he is married, to a woman named Beth. Pam has met her once, a shy, tall woman with a plain face—she played the game a half-dozen times, even winning once.

Pam knew from the first she appealed to Nolan. She learned long ago she appeals to most men. They had a cup of coffee out in the open, later a lunch in the shadows, then a drink that afternoon and a sly sneaking into his house from the rear basement door. She takes her seat at the table. Nolan won't look at her. Her head swims in dates and half-remembered cycles. She had thought she was between lovers and was using no contraception. Her calculations told her she was safe but she is not absolutely sure.

Getting settled, Owen shakes the dice, sips his beer, smokes, observes. Frank has his twenty red armies in five neat rows of four. Alice has rolled a joint thick as her little finger and touched a match lovingly to one twisted end. Blue smoke flows upward. A seed explodes and Pam jumps, laughs. Nolan grimaces.

Les counts out his twenty green armies. He is serene. The night, so clean and cold out on the highway, has purpose. He won the previous two times they played. He smiles idly around at those soon to fall. He asks Owen, "Did you buy that stock I told you about?"

"I don't have the money, Les."

"Get it. I went in at three and a half and it's seven already." He pauses to decline the joint Alice offers. "It's a great place for your money."

"I like banks," Frank says.

Les proclaims, "Banks are for suckers."

"They're insured," Frank says.

"So? You've got to go for the big return in this economy. Most people aren't chickenshit like you, Frank."

Owen, who as host strives for player equanimity, says mildly, "I still don't have the money."

Les shrugs. He can only do so much. He says, "Let's get this carnage under way."

Two red dice go around the table, each player rolling to see who goes first. With six players, the world's forty-two territories will be divided evenly. But the player who starts will be the first to have three cards (a card earned each turn if a territory is conquered), which he or she might be able to cash for extra armies.

Nolan's throw of ten is tops. Owen smiles and deals out the cards. They diverge from the rules in allotting territories. Each card represents a territory that a player will soon occupy with armies. Luck is involved, and time is saved. The players bring the cards up off the table, fan them in their hands, try to plot.

Les has been dealt New Guinea, and that is toehold enough for him on the continent of Australia. He deposits every available army there.

"A clear signal from Down Under," Nolan says. "Les is going for his continent early."

Les smiles beatifically.

Alice's seven territories are spread all over the world. She smokes her joint and studies her options. She knows that with six players, one or two will be eliminated early. A player without a firm base will be picked off a little at a time. Four of her territories are in Asia, which is much too large to try to hold as a continent. As she thinks, she feels herself float out of her seat; she feels her heels tap the chair seat as she rises clear. When she is on the ceiling, she lets out a laugh that is like taking on weight and drifts back down. Nobody has witnessed her brief ascension. They are too engrossed in the coming war. She sips wine and comes to a decision. She doesn't like Les very much when they play, and she owns Siam. It is the doorway to Asia from Australia, which Les will inevitably control. She puts all her armies in Siam.

Les looks over at her. She loves it when she makes his eyes go mean and flat. Les has green eyes, not as green as the color he plays, but green like dirty dollar bills. His eyes are always so cool and rich and calculating. He expects to win; this attitude rankles Alice no end. He may win tonight, but first he will have to fight through her.

Nolan has been splitting his armies between Central America and Greenland, preparatory to a run at North America. Seeing Alice's troop placement, he announces, "A bloodbath on the horizon in Siam."

Alice says, "I'm ready." Les drinks his wine.

"Les may want to invest in body bags," Frank says.

"I'm ready," Alice repeats.

Through all this, the only thing Owen hears is his wife moving in the room next to the kitchen. She has gone in there to get a book or the night's paper. She makes soft flutterings like a bird caught in the wall. He wishes she would come in, watch the game, have a glass of wine or a beer. An hour before the players arrived, they talked about having another baby. More than a year had passed, they were both in their early thirties, a better time would not arrive. But she could not give him an answer. Her willingness and her sadness remained locked together inside her.

Through the crack beneath the door he sees the light in the next room go out. He hears Eileen move deeper into the house, away from him; he thinks he hears her moving away long after the sounds have been hidden by the war around him.

Owen has Egypt, North Africa, and Madagascar, and he is delighted. He will soon control the continent of Africa. He won't be one of the first players eliminated, the host forced to sit and top off drinks and think.

Frank says cheerfully, "It's a gas to have the Middle East," and loads it full of his armies. He has nowhere else to go. His other armies are scattered in every continent, and worthless. He says, "The Middle East is the territory around which the world revolves."

"Frank's trying to sell himself a bill of goods," Les says.

"The poor jerk has nothing *but* the Middle East," Alice says.

Frank replies, "It's oily yet."

Pam owns Brazil and Venezuela, the doors in and out of the continent of South America. She divides her armies between the two territories.

"A bold move," Nolan announces. She looks to see if he is making fun of her, but his eyes trip away from hers.

The world is full of colored armies soon to contend. Nolan

begins. After placing his three free armies, he attacks Les's lone army in the Northwest Territory, loses an army before advancing, then loses another getting Owen out of Alaska.

"It's never easy," Nolan says. But he now controls the three routes in and out of North America. He takes his card. The game moves to Frank.

"Am I in danger?" Owen asks.

"Possibly," Frank says. He puts his three free armies in the Middle East.

"Because I want to go to the john."

"I just want to go for a card," Frank replies.

Owen leaves the kitchen. Let them wait for him if he can't get a straight answer. Eileen is in their bedroom. She sits against the headboard reading; she looks up almost warily when her husband appears.

"Who's winning?" she asks.

"Just started. Why don't you come out and say hello? Have a little wine."

His wife shakes her head. Her hair is a thick caramel wave that runs in and out of the light like surf. Her face is delicate and oval-shaped. He reads in her eyes that she expects the worst possible news at any moment. "I'd have to get dressed all over again," she explains. She's ready for sleep, in a flannel nightgown buttoned up the front and tied with a ribbon at the base of her throat. He kisses this spot, then uses the bathroom before returning to the game. Making his way down the shadowed hall, he glances into his house's second bedroom, but forces himself to think about getting hold of Africa instead.

Frank has darted into Southern Europe, taken his card, regrouped back in the Middle East, and stopped. Les has taken Australia. His armies wait in a clot in Indonesia, across a strait of blue-green water from Alice's Siamese force.

"The world is taking shape," Owen notes.

"Les suggests everyone invest in philatelic devices," Frank says.

"They're illegal in this state," Alice says.

Owen says nothing. He won't sit down just yet; not until it is his turn. He is unable to lose himself in the game. This has never been a problem. Tonight, though, he is itchy.

While he gets wine and beer and opens Pam's pretzels and pours them into a bowl, hosting the event in all earnestness, Pam takes South America. She and Les have continents, though they are the two continents easiest to win and hold, and hence worth only two bonus armies per turn. Still, they are continents. Les and Pam won't drift rootless over the world.

Alice's three free armies go into Siam. She looks at Les, her left eyebrow cocked, a question asked. He meets her look blankly. She sees that he has pushed his anger down. His cash-green eyes have reclaimed their arrogance.

Not yet, she decides. She attacks Nolan in India for her card, then pulls back into Siam.

"Buy body bags," Frank urges one and all. "Buy stock in the Red Cross."

Now Owen takes his seat. "Who has hot dice?" he asks.

"Nobody, really," Nolan reports. "Still too early. I think Alice should go after Les before his heat up."

"Les suggests we invest in numismatic tools," Frank says.

Owen rolls the dice against Pam and takes the Congo. His armies advance down through South Africa and up into East Africa. Just like that, Africa is his. He is spread too thin to hold it, he supposes, but he has a continent.

Nolan's turn again, and he can't remember what he wants to do next. Beth's face swims up to him, fitted on Pam's lush body. He stirs in his seat and tries to concentrate. He must fortify North America. One minute he was having a beer with Pam and the next he had come to this dangerous decision and they were parking her car a block over from his house. Cutting through the lawns, the darkening spaces between the houses, he could think only of the lack of cover. All the leaves were fallen; this was an affair meant for summer. He pulled the girl along by the hand. They went into the basement by the back door and undressed in the failing light. She tasted of flat beer when he kissed her for the first time. Chimes went off upstairs; he counted with them to five as he kissed her belly—an hour before Beth was due.

"Whose turn is it?" Les asks pointedly. Nolan's attention jerks back to the game. The world spreads before him. The girl keeps looking at him; she will give him away if she isn't careful. He is playing blue. Her sexual presence hit him the first time he saw her: a chemical lust. She never had to open her mouth. In fact, he preferred that she didn't. The peeling back of layers of existence that was life with Beth was never a factor with Pam. She was not very good at the game, and he knew nothing about her life otherwise. At their early meetings he filled the silent spaces talking about himself. He never thought about Beth at those times; she existed on a different plane. He found it remarkably easy to ask Pam to make that run to the basement with him. It would be the extent of what he wanted to know about her. Only when they were out in the open and on the run did it strike him what a wild chance he was taking.

And after they had been in the basement only twenty minutes, as they were finished and sitting in an awkward envelope of silence, a door opened above them and Beth's heels cracked smartly on the floor over their heads.

"Nolan," Les snarls, "it's too early in the game for such long thoughts."

Frank says, "It will be the rumination of your soul."

Nolan looks at Pam, then his eyes fly past. She waited with him in his basement like a canny burglar. Her ripe body had become an unwieldy burden he must transfer out of there for his own safety. His wife moved about upstairs, and the sky outside darkened. Then they slipped out the basement door and back to her car. She drove him to where he had left his car. They did not say a word, moving on those dark streets, as though his wife might yet hear. He took deep breaths to calm himself.

Leaving, he had looked back up at the house, and in the rectangle of light of the upstairs bedroom window he had thought he saw a woman looking out. But he had lost his glasses in the rush of adultery. He was flying blind. He had to be careful driving. At home he put on a spare pair and made a quick, surreptitious inspection of the basement. Nothing. No glasses. They were buried somewhere like a land mine. He might step on them at any moment and blow himself up. Beth, happy to see him, undressed and pulled him into bed with her. He said he didn't have time but she insisted; he noted no strangeness in her behavior, no knowledge of what he had done, of what he had become.

Owen gravely says, "As host, I'll have to rule you either move immediately, Nolan, or forfeit your turn."

Nolan slaps his three free armies down in Alaska. He conquers Les in Quebec from Greenland, then takes his card and sits back. Pam is a little disappointed. After such long consideration, she had expected something grand from Nolan.

"Bold," Les sneers.

"Jam it."

Frank drops more armies into the Middle East. Les says, "You can't let Owen keep Africa."

"Always fomenting trouble," Owen says good-naturedly. The possibility of attack hurries his blood, though. Frank moving on Egypt or East Africa is strategically sound. By the next turn, Owen will be better fortified. If he survives here, Africa will be his, probably for the entire game, with its three bonus armies per turn. Frank has the manpower at the moment and Owen's dice are rarely better than fair.

Frank attacks Owen in East Africa. Africa falls in six rolls of the dice. Les says, stirring more trouble, "You're poised to cut across North Africa and take South America away from Pam."

"No, thanks," Frank says. Too many armies wait in North Africa and Brazil. There is nothing in it for him. "I am content, not contentious," he says, and moves half his force back into the Middle East.

Les shakes Alice's shoulder, pretending she has fallen asleep. "You with us?" he asks in a loud voice. "Enough brain cells still alive to finish the game?"

She purses her lips as if to kiss and blows blue smoke in his face.

"I am ready," she says carefully, from the ceiling. These three words falling down to Les pull her after them like anchors. She wraps her leg around a leg of the table for balance and the table leg convulses. Les shrieks theatrically, "God! She's trying to get me sexually aroused so I'll go easy on her in Siam. But it won't work!"

He untangles his leg from Alice's. She grabs the table edge lest she float away again. A balloon of nausea rises in her. She puts her hand to her mouth and concentrates.

"Looking pale," Les says to the others, pointing at Alice.

"No fair throwing up on the world," Frank warns. "If you don't like your situation, be a man and live with it."

Les puts three armies in Indonesia, two in the Ukraine. He decides he is in no hurry. Let things build. He rolls the dice and there is a six. He gets a card from another point on the globe.

"Uh-oh," Frank says.

"Very efficient use of that six."

"Thank you," Les says modestly.

Alice smiles at them all. "It's early yet."

The world comes to Owen and it goes away. He is a fine host, and breaks out corn chips and roast-beef sandwiches, empties ashtrays, opens beers, pours wine. He spills liquids into the oceans and across the plains of Asia. The players groan and protest. A whale dives in the Mid-Atlantic. To the south, a tall ship moves under sail. He excuses himself. The light is out in their bedroom. It is 1:00 a.m., and Eileen sleeps in blankets wrapped tight as a premium cigar.

He passes the second bedroom going back and decides to go in. The crib had been dismantled right away. Even a year later the four indentations remain in the carpet where the casters pressed, stake holes for a precise parcel of ground. The baby had been so weightless, and home for such a short time; he is always amazed that she could mark the room so indelibly.

A night light remains in the wall socket. His wife might have overlooked it when she was cleaning out the room. She might have been afraid to look down. He kneels by it and snaps it on. A mouse's head, a glowing white face, round black ears, cartoon-rodent eyes. It's kind of unnerving: the head of a tiny ghost floating above the floor. Not the sort of thing for a baby girl. Had she been scared to death?

Owen returns to the game. Without Africa he is nothing, and the game has become a chore. He will be eliminated soon. Frank is gone already. Les took him out with the force he built in the Ukraine, using this secondary force to win cards and let some of the steam out of the situation brewing between Siam and Indonesia. Frank waited too long to take this Ukraine army seriously, and now he has gone outside; nobody knows what has happened to him.

Pam is pinned in South America. Owen's last armies block her in North Africa. Nolan has a major force in Central America. He will march on her in Venezuela.

The bloodbath between Alice and Les approaches. "You've got to come through me pretty soon," Alice taunts. "Nolan's getting too strong."

"This is a fact," Owen says. He desires resolution of this conflict so he can send his guests away.

The door opens and Frank is back.

"Where you been?"

"Standing naked in the dark," Frank says.

No one pays any attention. Nolan is attacking Pam. He goes after her in Venezuela, because it is the sound move at that point in the game, and also because he wants her gone. She usually leaves after she has been eliminated. Nights past, he was sorry to see her go. Now she embarrasses him. He expects her to slip up and start crying. She keeps looking at him.

Nolan rolls the dice and Pam waits. If he would look at her they might reach some understanding, but his eyes are fixed to that spot on the board where her dice will fall.

"Come on, come on," he says impatiently.

She rolls and loses two armies. Alice says, "Don't let him badger you."

"It's OK," Pam says softly. She thinks she will cry. Everything is wrong.

"Would you roll the dice?" he asks sharply.

She flings the dice across the board. She keeps them in sight through filmed eyes and sees sixes come up, which on closer inspection are really fours. Her tears make the pits shiver and drift. But fours are enough to win a pair of armies from Nolan, who rolls nothing higher than a three.

"Get him," Alice cheers.

But they are only dice; only Les has learned to tap their souls. Nolan's superior forces pick implacably away at Pam. Her armies fall like threads in a garment until they are all gone and she feels naked and stupid. Out of the game again. She turns her cards over to Nolan. He cashes them for extra armies and moves without a word against Owen in Africa. Pam watches this action blankly. She could open her mouth and tell everyone of the time she spent with Nolan in the recent past. She wields this knowledge like an ax on her tongue and is larger within herself for not using it.

She takes her empty glass and washes it out in the sink. At her back, Nolan eliminates Owen.

"You'll pardon me if I don't stay for the end," she says.

Owen stands, wipes his palms on his trousers. "I don't blame you for leaving," he says. "I'm bored myself."

"The pitiable whine of the previously conquered," Les observes dryly.

Owen smiles and takes Pam's coat off the tree and helps her into it. He walks her out to her car.

"Thanks for coming," he says. He likes being outside, away from the smoke and the bloodlust. The white gravel of his driveway gleams. The air feels like it wants to snow. He takes Pam's keys gallantly, and after she shows him the one, he unlocks her car door. Owen leans in and kisses her good night. She hands him a pair of glasses.

"They belong to the guy playing blue," she says. "I saw him downtown today and we had coffee together and he left them with me by mistake."

These words break over Owen in a rush; he can only say, "OK."

He stays outside after Pam is gone. Nolan's car is unlocked; he puts the glasses on the dash. He has no interest in the truth of their coming into Pam's possession. He returns to his house through the front door. He hears the voices of the players in the kitchen, the labored buzz of an old digital clock turning a minute over. Through the dark passages of the house, moving with a freedom bestowed by his guests' believing he is still outside, Owen glides into the bedroom. His wife lies wrapped and asleep. He understands now why the night's game offered him nothing; it was an event out of order of importance. Eileen comes half awake at the way he pulls the covers and makes a space for himself in the loose, warm cylinder. He gets her nightgown unbuttoned and untied and fights through the clumsy hands she throws in his path. He plants a long kiss on her sour mouth. She utters a word into his mouth that he ignores. She will kill his desire if he lets her.

"Where are your friends?" she whispers, warm in his ear.

"In the kitchen. The world will fall soon."

"You aren't being a good host." He is stirred unimaginably to hear teasing in her voice. Her hands have opened against his back.

"They think I'm outside," he whispers. "This way, I can be two places at once."

She kisses him on the neck. They move on together, Owen careful of dark chasms of memory he must transport his wife over. She proceeds along a fine edge that her husband slowly widens.

Les says, "Siam from China."

"Hand me the bones, please," Alice says. Frank gives her the white dice. "Like skulls," she says, "with twenty-one lance holes."

"Siam from China," Les repeats.

"Pincer movement," Nolan announces.

"Pinch her movement and she'll follow you anywhere," says Frank.

Les has swept his second force into China so he can attack Alice's Siamese armies from both north and south. He rolls dice the same way from first to last: three shakes of his left fist, then a gentle, coddling tipping of the dice out onto the board, as though they might bruise. It is his secret that he treats the dice well so they will reciprocate. He once revealed this secret while drunk and voluble, and seven straight games of cold dice followed as punishment.

He beats on Alice from China: a softening action. Alice is poised for defeat. He can see in her slack face that she has had enough: enough grass, enough of their company, enough of this game. She is tired and anxious to go home.

"Where's Owen?" Nolan asks.

"He walked Pam to her car," Frank says.

"That was a half-hour ago."

"So?" Les asks, impatient at this break in his concentration. "Go look for him if you're so concerned. But shut up."

"Gee, Les, you're such a charming guy," Frank says.

"Eat it."

"Come on, Les," Alice complains. "Roll the dice. I wanna go home."

"The night is breaking up in a sea of bad juices," Frank says. "Why does it always have to be this way? Like love."

"Shut up, Frank."

Nolan is at the window, cupping hands around his eyes to see through the light reflected on the glass. Chrome winks from the handlebars of Les's motorcycle. He can see Alice's car, his car, Frank's car. Not Pam's car, though.

"They left together," he says.

"Who did?" Frank asks.

"Pam and Owen."

"No way," Alice says.

"Intriguing, though," Les admits.

"Her car is gone. So is Owen. You put it together."

"He's married," Frank says.

"Frank, you're such an innocent," Alice says.

Frank says, "And his wife is in the other room. Who'd have the nerve to go off with another woman under those conditions?"

Nolan says, "Maybe she's asleep. Maybe he figures she figures he's still out here. She never checks on him. Maybe he figured it was worth the gamble."

"Are we still playing?" Alice asks Les. He is startled; he has been thinking about Pam. The dice feel funny in his hand, as though the corners have been shaved fractionally, or the pits rearranged. They feel cool at being ignored in the midst of their performance for him. He is afraid to roll, and when he does it's all ones and twos. He rolls cold for the next five minutes, losing armies, losing confidence. In time his China force is wiped out, and Alice still exists firmly in Siam. Outnumbered, she nonetheless has the hot dice that ordinarily are his province, as though they have taken another lover. Fives and sixes roll languorously from her hand. Alice licks her lips, wide awake now. Hot dice get everyone's attention. Les awaits her exclamation of disbelief in her good fortune, which will drive the dice spitefully back to him. But it does not come. He loses armies in pairs. By and by, they are evenly matched, Siam and Indonesia, and Les stalls to count armies, trying to cool her dice this way.

Nolan says, "I feel uncomfortable without a host." He opens himself a fresh beer. He begins to look through bills that Owen keeps stacked on the counter next to the telephone.

"Jesus, Owen has $1,108 on his Visa," he informs the others.

"Stop that," Alice scolds.

Les likes this unexpected turn; Nolan's rude exploration has taken Alice's mind off the game.

"Many people are faced with serious and potentially cata- strophic debt," Les says.

Nolan goes on. "A phone bill for $79.21."

"What if Owen comes back and finds you doing that?" Alice asks. When her head is turned away from Les, he blows gently toward the dice in her hand to cool them.

"He's with Pam," Nolan says. Saying this makes it a fact; makes him feel released.

"Roll the dice," Les orders. "I want to get out of here before daylight." He is certain that the dice have come back to him. Alice has lingered too long between throws. She has lost favor by ignoring the good fortune that the dice were eager to bestow. He reminds her, "I'm still attacking."

Alice rolls, thinking of Owen. He had telephoned her when the baby died, the phone seeming to explode with compressed tragedy in the middle of the night. To this day, she can't talk to Eileen without seeing grief encasing her like an invisible jar. Only lately has Alice seen her smile. Would Owen go off with Pam at just such a time?

Les wins two armies. Then two more.

Nolan says, "A bill for $177.44 from People's Gas."

Alice wishes Owen would return and discover Nolan and banish him forever. But the house is silent except for the click of dice. Maybe Owen *has* left with Pam; maybe it is the only response to this time in history. The man Alice meets on the sly is married to a sweet woman who he claims has nothing of interest to say. And Alice has never considered herself fascinating. The man she shares the farmhouse with had a marriage end years ago when he was caught in a hammock with another woman. She thinks this might make her safe, that he might understand if he ever catches her.

Les rolls and Alice falls. He was right: the dice have come back. When he clears her out of Siam, he still has ten armies in Indonesia. He takes the four cards Alice holds, and with the cards already in his hand cashes twice for forty-five armies, a huge green force he places with care to battle Nolan while his dice are running hot. It takes another hour to finish the game. The dice are at home in Les's loosely cupped fist and at two minutes to four o'clock in the morning he is the winner for the third consecutive time. Alice and Frank sit quietly and watch.

"Dear Les," Alice says, standing and stretching. "You do go on."

"And on . . . and on," Frank says. "Like a fungus." He shakes Les's hand. He folds Owen's board, puts the cards away, puts the armies in their containers.

Nolan asks, "Did Owen take his key?"

"I couldn't tell you," Les says.

"If we lock the door," Frank says, "and he has to knock to get in, we could be inadvertently exposing him to exposure. Or exposure. A guy like Owen could die of exposure."

"He should've thought of that," Nolan says.

"He can just say he forgot it," Les says. "He could say he went to breakfast after the game and forgot it."

Alice puts the wine in the refrigerator and washes out the glasses. She leaves a small light on over the stove.

Birds stir outside, though it is still dark. The four of them stand, corners of a square, in the driveway.

"Somebody mentioned breakfast," Nolan says.

Frank pats his pockets. "I'm broke."

"I'll buy," Nolan says. "The vanquished will buy with the reparations they receive from the victors."

"Ha! You'll get nothing from me," Les says.

"I'll still buy."

"I think I'll pass," Alice says.

"You'll pass on a free meal?"

"I don't feel so hot."

"Suit yourself," Frank says.

The other three turn from her and make their plans. She does not want to be alone just then, though a sleeping man who loves her awaits at the end of the drive home. Nolan and Frank start their cars and drive off and she is left standing there with Les. He sits astride his motorcycle, pulling on his gloves and watching her.

"Come with us," he urges.

She moves to his side. "I'm tired of Nolan and Frank." She kisses Les. "Can't we go somewhere?"

He laughs. "That might be difficult to explain. I've been coming and going at awfully odd hours. She thinks I play this game at all hours of the day and night."

"Coward."

Owen is awakened by Les's motorcycle starting. Unwinding himself from Eileen, he feels her stir. She loops an arm around his waist when he sits up on the edge of the bed. His friends will be going for breakfast at this early hour. It is a tradition of the game. The night's war will be replayed. Stories will be told, rumors will be spread. Owen would love to go with them, but he doesn't dare.

Arcadia

Arcadia comes toward Sutton talking, talking, with that lovable grin and that mouthful of dazzling teeth, and Sutton hasn't a clue what is being said.

They work together on a mountain of bricks. One building has come down, another is going up. The old bricks are better than new, sturdy and valuable. Their job is to find whole bricks among the cracked and stack them at the foot of the mountain.

Arcadia is good at this work. He is like a dancer on this brick mountain, finding good bricks, arranging them carefully along his forearm, stepping down to add them to the rest. He works in old leather boots his little toes show through.

Sutton can only guess that Arcadia is proud of his perfect teeth, he displays them so much. Behind these teeth is a pink point of tongue that creates long incoherent stretches of sound. His smiling eyes, curly hair, white teeth, his pure happy countenance, make Arcadia a hit with the ladies at lunch. All the men on the job gather at a restaurant down the street and Arcadia talks, talks. He talks and smiles and the girls just appear. Sutton wonders, Do they understand what he is saying? Does Arcadia speak some code of love?

Sutton has a smile of his own on his face. He guesses it looks pretty false; it feels false. But through the incomprehensibility of Arcadia's words comes a love of life Sutton envies. He suspects this quality alone would bring the girls around. He would hate for Arcadia to think Sutton did not love life as much.

So Sutton listens and smiles. He listens to the cadence of Arcadia's jabbering and produces a frozen laugh when he thinks a punch line has been delivered or a point made. He looks Arcadia straight in the eye and laughs to celebrate their common love of life.

Sutton stops Zeeland where they can talk in private. Zeeland is always laughing and chattering with Arcadia; he is a fun-loving guy who grabs the seat next to Arcadia every day at lunch. Sutton envies Zeeland because he seems so attuned.

"How long did you know Arcadia before you understood him?" Sutton asks.

"I understood him from Day One."

"You did?"

"Sure. What's not to understand?"

"Everything. Everything that comes out of his mouth is a mystery to me. I couldn't even tell you the language he speaks."

Zeeland says, "You got it all wrong, Sutton. I didn't say I understand what he's saying. I said I understand *him*. I sit next to him because that's where all the girls will be."

"But you talk to him," Sutton says.

"Sure. I'm no stiff. He's got no more idea what I'm saying than I've got what he's saying. We're both after the same thing. Just smile and get your two cents in. That's all any of us try to do."

Arcadia holds a brick in front of him with both hands. He is smiling, his eyes flashing black, his voice musical and baffling. As Sutton watches, Arcadia breaks the brick in two by slamming it against his forehead. Sutton is amazed. But it's only a trick.

The brick was in two pieces held together to look like one. Arcadia laughs and performs the trick again. Brick dust clings to his forehead. He takes the broken brick to lunch and delights the girls with it.

When the men return to work Sutton hangs back and says to one of the girls, "Nice fella, Arcadia." He wants to turn on his smile like Arcadia, sound the charm gong, but there is nothing there and it shows in the girl's face. He talks to her because she is among the prettiest of them.

"Who?" she asks.

"Arcadia." Sutton points to the man's spot; Arcadia sits in the same seat every day, smiling king of that domain.

"You work with him?" she asks.

"Sure. We're good friends."

"He's always got a smile."

"One for everyone," Sutton agrees. "You ever date him?"

Her eyes flash up at Sutton. He has broken through her disinterest in the wrong way. "None of your business," she snaps, "even if I had."

Arcadia's car reminds Sutton of Arcadia's work boots; there are brick-sized rust holes he expects Arcadia's feet to show through. Arcadia is often the last to leave at the end of the day. He laughs and chatters, trying to get his car to start. Each man sounds his horn as he drives past and Arcadia always looks up and grins and waves goodbye. Arcadia is also often the first man at work in the morning.

Arcadia lives somewhere away from work. Sutton wonders if he has been told where and didn't realize it. He might have been invited over and accepted the invitation and not shown up.

Zeeland says, "I saw him downtown once. He saw me first and came right up to me. Talking a mile a minute. I talked right back to him. We each bought a round of beers. A great guy. Nothing but women hanging all over him."

"Did they talk to him?"

"Hell, Sutton, everybody talked to him. You're too stiff. Everybody says that about you. Loosen up. Be sociable for once in your life."

Arcadia returns from an errand, talking, talking, and scrambles up the brick mountain to where Sutton works. Sutton smiles into Arcadia's beaming face. The happy words, Arcadia's moist breath, break over Sutton's false face. He's being sociable, he thinks; he wants to be. But he can't loosen up enough to comment or respond to something that baffles him.

Instead, he says, "What?"

Arcadia stops talking. He doesn't stop smiling, only talking. The bricks clink beneath their feet.

Sutton says, "I don't understand you."

Arcadia talks for a moment, smiling hopefully at Sutton.

"I'm sorry," Sutton says. "I've got no idea what you're saying."

Arcadia talks through his smile, talking, talking.

"Stop. Stop," Sutton says. "I don't know how to tell you this, but all the time I've worked with you and laughed at what I think were jokes, I haven't had the faintest idea what you were saying. I haven't understood a single word."

Arcadia laughs, scratches his head, taps one of his big front teeth. He talks, talks, and Sutton gives up and goes back to sorting bricks. He looks for Zeeland after work but Zeeland is quick leaving at the end of the day in ways totally unrelated to his pace of work.

The men leave in a hurry, they honk at Arcadia, who smiles and waves back. In minutes Sutton is alone in the lot with Arcadia and his car, which won't start. He grinds the ignition, talking, talking to himself, and the picture so frustrates Sutton he hasn't the courage to offer to help and speeds away without looking back.

It rains hard all night. Sutton and Arcadia are taken off the brick mountain, given buckets and shovels and high boots, and sent inside where neither the roof nor the floor has been completed. The floor is mud, and beneath those sections of the roof that remain uncovered a million little lakes have formed. Their new job is to drain this ground.

Arcadia does not share Sutton's sense of their task's ridiculousness. He works like a civil engineer or a child at the beach cutting canals with his shovel blade so one lake can run into another. From these larger pools he delicately shovels the water into the bucket, and when the bucket is full he carries it across the muddy floor, outside to a hill, and flings it down where there is no chance of its ever running back inside. Arcadia has the perfect temperament for this job. He seems to draw pride and bottomless delight from slowly shoveling a shallow keystone of water on the blade of a shovel up and into a bucket while spilling a third to a half of his original cargo. Nothing upsets him.

Sutton can't get the hang of it. His canals are only wet trails in the mud. They don't consolidate any significant amounts of water. And the act of shoveling water is just too ludicrous for words.

At lunch he sits by himself in his muddy clothes, listening to Arcadia's happy chatter and the echoing bleats of Zeeland and all the others. Girls appear as if conjured. There is nobody but the men from work and then Arcadia talks, talks, and girls are present. There is camaraderie, low-grade flirting, an exchange of desires.

Arcadia walks with Sutton back to where their buckets and shovels wait. Sutton ignores everything Arcadia says now. He has made his point; he is free to be himself.

Sutton sees no improvement in the ground they have gone over. A million lakes remain. It could rain again that night and set them back to the start. This does not seem to bother Arcadia.

Even more than picking through bricks, digging canals and draining tiny lakes hold a real charm for him.

When the whistle blows at five o'clock Arcadia reluctantly turns in his shovel and bucket and high boots. He goes to his car and gets in, but he does not try to start it. As the rest of the men sweep past out of the parking lot, honking, waving, Arcadia doesn't wave, doesn't smile, doesn't look at any of them.

Sutton drives away, too. But after dinner he keeps thinking about Arcadia and his life away from work. It is a short drive back and when he arrives Arcadia's car is still in the lot. Sutton finds him stretched out in the back seat. He has his socks off and rolled into a small pillow. He is reading a newspaper in a nest of fast-food wrappers; he sucks the last of his shake with a straw.

Sutton taps on the window. Arcadia lowers the paper. A big smile breaks across his face. He starts talking, talking, even as he pulls on his socks and boots and gets out of the car.

"You live in your car," Sutton says.

Arcadia laughs, shrugs, talks. He locks his car door and gets into Sutton's car, his arms loaded with dirty clothes, old newspapers, a pair of work gloves.

They move out onto the highway. Arcadia points toward the city.

"I tell you," Sutton says. "I've got no idea what you're saying or where I'm going."

Arcadia points, laughs. The sun is going down and Sutton wants to be home. Arcadia seems to have a destination. Through his happy jabbering he directs Sutton onto links of highway that stretch toward the city, then through the city, then out the other side. He leads Sutton down streets between bunched buildings that thin like the light until it is dark and nobody, nothing, is around.

Sutton thinks he sees the state line flash past on the edge of his headlights. Arcadia is truly happy now. At a stop sign he points right and two blocks on he points left. He tells Sutton to stop at a tiny house in the middle of the block.

Arcadia is out of the car while it is still rolling. He runs up the driveway with his armload of belongings. An outside light goes on. A pretty little girl with Arcadia's dark curly hair and jabbering tongue bursts out the door and sprints toward him. She hits the things in Arcadia's arms like they were a cloud meant to catch her. A short, voluptuous woman follows the little girl. This woman is cross, but too happy to sustain it. Her wide hips and bowed legs swing like a gunfighter's as she advances on Arcadia, who faces her squarely and gives her a long kiss and a smack on the rump. They all talk, talk, and Arcadia turns to wave Sutton into their net.

The little girl takes Sutton's arm. He is pulled into the house like a hero. The woman clears laundry from a chair and the little girl pulls him into it. There is barely room for all of them in the kitchen. The girl has been doing arithmetic at the table. Dinner was over long ago but the woman goes to work fixing a meal for Sutton and Arcadia. She talks, talks.

Sutton feels obliged to say, "I've got no idea what you're talking about."

No one listens. The woman and the girl are intent on Arcadia. Sutton looks at the girl's arithmetic. He is afraid it is in the alien tongue the family converses in; he fears he has wandered into another world entirely.

But the girl's work is clearly earthling. Her numbers are carefully put down in pencil on sheets of manila paper perforated to tear free from the workbook. Sutton even sees two problems done incorrectly. He will have to leave them be. How could he ever explain them to her?

A blue porcelain plate full of pork chops, niblet corn, and buttered rolls is placed before him. The woman beams down on him, talking, talking. She pours coffee. She's a beautiful woman. Sutton senses springiness in everything about her; her happy manner, the coiled wires of her hair, the swing of her body in her thin housedress. Sutton is envious of Arcadia and sees him in a new light. He wonders why he made no more effort to get home to this woman, dead car or not.

The woman is out of the room for a few minutes and reappears to remove the dirty plates. Arcadia yawns. He has talked all through dinner, fitting his words haphazardly around the food in his mouth. Now he runs his hands down the front of his shirt, unbuttoning as he goes, and Sutton gets the hint. It is a long way home and he has no idea how to get there.

The little girl appears, washed and ready for bed. She carries a limp toy rabbit in the crook of her arm. Her mother has bound her hair in two thick sheaves atop her head. Sutton is kissed on the cheek, Arcadia on the lips, and the girl is off to bed.

Sutton is looking for his jacket when the woman takes his arm. She says a few words. He follows her into the next room, where a bed has been made for him on a couch. TV light spills over the turned sheets, blanket, pillow, making them look soiled.

The woman talks, talks, Sutton can't bear to look at her. The house pinches in on him and this woman and Arcadia. Already he hears the gentle rhythm of the little girl's sleep. It passes effortlessly through the house. He does not think he can lie on this narrow bed and listen to Arcadia and his wife reunited after untold nights apart. He hears the water running in the shower, Arcadia singing, singing.

But Sutton has no choice.

He undresses in the dark and slides into the cool bedding. Out the room's only window he sees a red light beating high in the distance, a warning to planes.

He thinks he sleeps, but he can't be sure. He is awake now. The small house is quiet but for three rhythms of sleep. The red light pulses on, the darkness at its back subtly different, a half-shade lighter, or darker, he can't say.

There is nothing for him to do but dress and sit at the window, waiting to take Arcadia back.

Sofa Art

Fran was shown to a chair alongside the teacher's desk. "Mr. Reese couldn't come?" Mr. Frobel asked.

"He has a show tonight."

"I've forgotten what it is he shows."

"He manages wholesale art exhibitions," Fran said. "He's in Merrillville tonight, tomorrow, and Sunday."

"Is that what they call couch art?" he asked, with a twist to his mouth to indicate that he knew otherwise.

"Sofa art," she said. "Stephen calls them stain blockers."

The teacher laughed, and as he laughed he opened a file bearing her son's name. "I'm sorry Mr. Reese couldn't be here," Mr. Frobel said. "I've started holding these conferences in the evenings in order that both parents can attend. I've been surprised by all the people who work nights."

"He wanted to be here," Fran said. "He won't be home until three this morning."

"People actually buy that stuff?"

"Oh, yes. That sort of art is very popular."

Mr. Frobel was reading while Fran spoke. When she finished, he began. "Teddy is still having problems," he said. "I touched on some of these at our earlier conference. Basically, nothing has changed. He's twelve years old. I regard it as a bridge age—not a kid anymore but before adolescence really sets in. I think Teddy is at a very critical juncture in his development."

"How have his grades been?" Fran asked.

Mr. Frobel shrugged and turned a page. "Middling. Mediocre. If the cards came out tomorrow, he'd have mostly C's and D's."

"B's?" she asked.

"No, *D's*. But you miss the point by concentrating on grades. They're merely a sign of something deeper. It's my impression Teddy just doesn't give a damn—excuse me, a hoot. He wants to do well to please you and Mr. Reese, to please me, but that only goes so far. I don't think he's interested in pleasing himself. I—*we*—haven't been able to touch that part of him. He's a bright boy, he's got friends. But he doesn't concentrate. He daydreams. Bluntly, your son is a goof."

When Fran got home, she expected Teddy to be in his room studying, because he knew where she had been and he also knew that Mr. Frobel's report would not be good. She knocked once on the door and it swung open, which was a surprise—it was usually shut and locked these days. Teddy wasn't there.

In the kitchen, she poured some tea into a glass, added ice, and looked out the window to see if Teddy was in the back yard. He and his friends often played a game they called guerrilla football there at night. They wore dark clothing, there were no teams, there was no talking, and the ball could be anywhere. But the yard was empty. "Teddy?" Fran called loudly.

His faint answer came from a room at the opposite end of the house—a drafty little greenhouse that the previous owners had added. They had done the work on the cheap, and the windows leaked when it rained and when the winter snow melted. Fran could often find her husband in that room when he was home. He said he liked the light there. Stephen considered himself a painter, though he was always reading when she looked in on him. A painting on the easel by the wall was evidently of something outside the windows which he alone could see.

She found Teddy sitting beneath her husband's drawing table, reading by flashlight. Even after she entered the room and stood facing him, he did not move. His stillness seemed to imply a wish that she did not know where he was and might go away.

"Come out," she said. "I want to have a talk with you, mister."

His emergence was an elaborate juggling of the flashlight, the book, his height, and a blue blanket he clasped around his shoulders. When he stood, the top of her head reached to just below his eyes. "Mom," he said. The toes of his white socks were stained with pastel chalk dust. "Where's Dad tonight?"

"In Merrillville, as you know."

"You'd think they'd run out of that stuff."

"I saw Mr. Frobel tonight," she said. "I didn't like what he had to say one bit."

"I'll try harder," Teddy said.

"You always say that, but you never seem to do it. Mr. Frobel said you're only getting C's and D's. You're smarter than that. And what about that map of Russia? How far along are you?"

"I've still got some work to do on it."

"Let me see what you've done."

"I left it at school," Teddy said. "I'll bring it home Monday and show you."

"It's *due* Monday."

"It is?"

"*Teddy!* Have you even started it?"

"I've looked up a few of the places."

"Do you have the list here?"

"It's in my locker. I can remember most of the stuff Frobel wanted."

"Name some of the cities."

"Moscow . . . Leninville."

"Lenin*grad*. How about the mountain ranges?"

"The *Orals*," he said with a proud snarl. "The—"

"Teddy. Sit." Fran took a mimeographed sheet from her pocket. It was the list of Russian place names that were to be included on the map. Mr. Frobel had given it to her as she left the room, possibly because he knew Teddy Reese better than his mother thought he did. "You get started on this map right away," she said. "And don't go out of the house or turn on the TV until it's finished. Do you understand?"

"*Mom.*"

"That's it, Teddy. And it's the Urals, not the Orals, you goof."

They both lay listening in their own way for Stephen's return. Teddy resented the sleep he was losing because of his father's absence—he wouldn't get to talk to him, and it was unlikely he would hear anything of his mother's report. But he couldn't go to sleep without the comforting, subdued racket of his father's safe arrival. Before going to bed, he had begun the map. He had taped two heavy sheets of white paper side by side, and almost immediately smudged a thumbprint across one corner. He erased it. The atlas was open. He worked for a long time drawing the border of Russia.

Fran kept thinking she heard Stephen. She knew the sounds—car, keys, lock, footsteps, jingling, sighs. His shape would fill the bedroom doorway. Usually, whether she spoke or pretended to be asleep depended on her mood, because she didn't know which he preferred. But tonight she had already decided to tell him about the visit with Teddy's teacher. She was excited, sensing something had unaccountably gone right in her handling of the situation. It was late, but she suppressed the desire to sleep. She had to talk to him now, because he would be gone when she awakened.

She wondered what the painting in the studio was supposed to be. More than a year ago, Stephen had brought home an expensive array of art supplies with the intention of becoming a painter. "I can do better than this crap," he said, slapping a piece of sofa art that he had brought home to show her. It was a Venetian scene. The painting's back was electrically wired, and tiny lights burned in the windows of the houses and in the gondolas' lanterns. "It's the newest thing," he went on. "Plug-in sofa art. They're working on battery-powered sofa art. Solar-powered sofa art is ten years in the future."

There. Teddy heard him. Noises from the front of the house left no doubt that his father was home. It was one minute after three. His father deposited his keys and change in the candy dish on the shelf in the kitchen. Next would come the clunk of his dropped shoes. He'd fill a glass with ice and draw water from the tap. Finally, he would begin his patrol of the house to make certain his wife and son had survived his absence.

Teddy wanted to call to his father when he looked into the room. He wanted to assure him that the situation was not as bad as his mother was going to make it sound. Look at the map of Russia. The border was in. Moscow. Minsk. Omsk. Tashkent. Each in its place. Much remained to be done, but it was going to be all right. But he only peeked at Stephen through the slit of an eye. His father was a thick shadow with the light at his back. He murmured something Teddy couldn't understand, then moved on.

Fran rolled over to signal that she was awake. Stephen sighed and sat on the edge of the bed. Then he gently toppled back, his head landing perfectly in the firm hollow at her center. Her fingers felt for his hair. "I'm glad you're home," she whispered. "How'd it go?"

"The artistic taste of Merrillville is improving," he said. "We didn't sell much." He laughed softly. The shiver of his laughter was electric against her. "Let me tell you about one painting," he said. "The horizontal sword-swallower. It's five feet wide. A yard high. A skinny guy lying on his back with a sword in his mouth. He's getting ready to put another one in. We just got this one today. Buckets of black, red, and silver paint went into this masterpiece. It's worth a hundred dollars just for the petroleum by-products. Tomorrow, he goes up to $125. We'll make an event out of him. We didn't get one nibble tonight. People were laughing at him."

"Did you sell anything?"

"The four-dollar items. Big-eyed clowns. Matadors. Kittens. Elvis."

She smoothed his eyebrows with a fingertip. "I had my conference with Teddy's teacher tonight," she said.

"And?"

"He said Teddy's still having problems. Mr. Frobel said Teddy wants to please *us*. But he doesn't care if he pleases himself. He daydreams. He has a lot of friends. But he's a goof."

"Is that an accepted educational term now? *Goof?*"

"He doesn't pay attention," she said. "He doesn't try unless he thinks it will please someone else. He's got no sense of himself being important."

"Hell, I daydreamed," her husband said. "It usually means the teacher is a bore. Frobel ever consider that?"

Fran touched Stephen's face and it was surprisingly cool—he sounded so angry.

"How are his grades?" he asked.

"Mr. Frobel said they were mediocre. C's and D's."

"You and I both know Teddy's not mediocre."

"Mr. Frobel told me about an assignment he'd given the class," Fran said. "They have to draw a map of Russia."

"You mean the Soviet Union. Nobody calls it Russia anymore."

"Is that important? May I finish?"

"Yes, you can finish."

"He handed out a sheet listing cities, rivers, seas, mountain ranges—everything you could imagine—and the kids are supposed to have all these places on their maps," she said. "I came home and asked to see Teddy's. He said he'd left it at school, that I could see it Monday. Well, the damn thing's *due* Monday, and he had no idea."

"Did Frobel blame me?" Stephen asked.

"Blame you?"

"Because I wasn't there? Because I was working? Did he blame Teddy's problems on my absences?"

She was angry at him for missing the point and trying to make it his crisis. "Mr. Frobel did remark on your not being there," she said. "He said he was surprised at the number of people who work nights."

"We're an entire subculture. Like bugs under rocks."

"I told Teddy he can't go out of the house this weekend," she said. "He has to work on the map until it's finished."

"Isn't that a little unbending?" her husband asked.

Stephen was gone when Teddy awoke. His mother remained asleep. In the kitchen, he poured apple juice and buttered six slices of toast, then covered three with peanut butter and three with grape jelly. He took his breakfast to his bedroom. He returned to the kitchen for a stack of paper napkins. He didn't want to get stains on his map. For a long time he ate and studied what he had accomplished. The map, rolled the night before into a protective tube, now had to be weighted at the corners. The border was not quite as well done as he had thought it was. Erasures gleamed. A stone of discouragement settled in his chest. He had so much to do and so little chance of getting it absolutely right. Teddy wished he could have spoken to his father before he left. He came and went so fast. Teddy would again be in bed when his father came home, and he would again be asleep when he left the next morning.

Teddy found the Caspian Sea in the atlas and labeled it on his map. He made a checkmark alongside "Caspian Sea" on the mimeographed sheet. Was he half finished? More than half? The satisfaction of beginning the project had dissipated. Now it was just Saturday morning, the sun was out, and he had to do this map.

"How's it going?"

Fran was in the doorway; Teddy jumped when she spoke. "You *scared* me," he said.

"Sorry," she said. She went to the desk but didn't lower her eyes to look at the map. "Did you talk to Daddy this morning?" she asked.

"He was gone when I woke up."

"He's always on the go when there's a show to do," she said. "But he'll be home tomorrow night."

"And all next week we won't be able to get rid of him."

She laughed and mussed his hair.

"Did you tell him about meeting with Mr. Frobel?"

"Of course I did."

"Was he mad?"

"I don't know," she said. "He's such a big fan of yours— he doesn't think you're capable of doing anything wrong."

When he looked away in bewilderment, she glanced down at the map, then turned away from the desk. Was the map as good as it had looked in that instant's examination? "If you fail, he blames himself," she said.

"*If* I fail?"

"If. When. Don't be so hard on yourself. I'm going to fix myself some breakfast. When do I get to see the map?"

"When it's finished. And maybe not then."

Eva Hooks called that afternoon and invited Fran over for coffee. Eva was a substitute teacher, with four children of her own. She often remarked how sweet Teddy was—how both of her daughters had a crush on him. "I'll lace it with brandy," she promised.

"I'm sort of overseeing Teddy," Fran said. "He's been grounded to work on a school project. I'd feel bad deserting him."

"Who's grounded, him or you? He'd probably be relieved to have you out of the house."

"Well, maybe I will stop by for a while."

Fran could reach Eva's house by cutting through the hedge at the rear of the back yard. Teddy watched his mother's progress until she stepped through the Hookses' back door.

Fran stayed until the light was nearly gone. When she came back through the hedge, the yard was full of stalking shadows unaware of her presence. She could not pick Teddy out from among the boys playing guerrilla football.

Someone materialized at her side and said, "Hello, Mrs. Reese." It was one of Teddy's friends, and he was smiling at her. His face was painted with something black. "Teddy told us he was grounded, but he said it would be OK if we played out here," the boy went on. "You have the perfect yard—all these trees and bushes."

With a hiss the football struck him in the neck and he dropped at her feet. He feigned injury while his hands searched the ground for the ball. She looked down and saw that he was still smiling.

Teddy's room was empty. The map was held down at the corners.

"Teddy?" she called. "Teddy?"

He answered from the bathroom.

"Aren't those kids out there bothering you?"

"No."

"How's the map going?"

"Great."

"Come out where I can look at you."

"Jesus, Mom. When I'm done."

"I'll talk to you later, then. I'm going to lie down for a bit," she said.

"OK."

Teddy waited another ten minutes before he went out of the bathroom. His face stung where he had scrubbed it clean. The knees of his black corduroys were shiny with smeared grass. He'd figured that his mother wouldn't wait outside the bathroom door. Soft snores rose from her on the sofa in the den. His friends were gone. He turned on a couple of lights to cheer up the house and returned to the map.

Stephen had departed when Fran was asleep, and now he returned when she was in her nightshirt, in bed again. She might never have moved. "I hate weekends," she whispered when he came into the bedroom.

"Tell me about it," he said. He lay down on the bed on his back, one hand on her stomach, one hand over his eyes.

"How was it?" Fran asked.

"A good day. We sold a bunch."

"The horizontal sword-swallower?"

"No. Nibbles, though. One family, I thought I had them. The mom sort of resembled the guy in the picture."

Fran put a hand over her laugh.

"But I think the price finally turned them off," he said. "It was too *low*. If it was outrageously expensive, they could justify its stupidity by its high price. That makes it *art*."

"Do you have to leave so early again tomorrow? Teddy wants to talk to you."

"He sleeps too late."

"What time do you have to leave?"

"Nine, quarter after. I'll be back by ten tonight, though."

"His map is turning out wonderfully," Fran said. "He hasn't shown it to me, but I've snuck glimpses. It looks—*professional*."

"We can frame it and hang it over the couch," he said. She lightly punched his shoulder.

She felt him relax. His breathing stretched out, and he

seemed to lengthen and settle into the mattress. In a minute, he was asleep.

Stephen was gone by eight the next morning.

"Daddy wanted to talk to you," Fran told Teddy in the kitchen. "He'll talk to you tonight."

"He's a rumor," Teddy said.

"He works very hard. Part of that means he's away a lot."

"It's the *weekend*."

"He has a strange schedule. Don't forget that he's home a lot when other dads are at work."

"And I'm in school."

"He wants to hang your map of Russia."

Teddy blinked. The map was finished. He was afraid to show it to his mother, however. She might not think it was as good as he thought it was.

"Are you kidding?" he asked.

"That's what he said."

"He hasn't even seen it."

"He has faith in you. He knows you'll do a good job."

"He was teasing," Teddy said. "He's always teasing. He's so sarcastic."

"I think he meant it."

"Where would we hang it?"

"How big is it?"

He shaped the dimensions with his hands. Doing so, he saw the map in almost complete detail. Kirgiz Steppe. Tarko-Sale. Laptev Sea. Gulf of Ob. He had found every one, and marked them all.

"Maybe in the studio," she said. "Or in your room."

"Out of the way, in other words," Teddy said.

Fran rolled her eyes. "Or over the couch?"

"It's finished," he said quickly. "I've finished the map."

"You have? That's wonderful! Can I see it?"

"Can I go out? Am I still grounded?"

"What about your other homework?"

"I'll do it later."

"May I see the map?"

"Later," Teddy said, and he was gone before his mother could retract the consent he had read in her eyes.

She washed the dishes and wiped the kitchen counter. The quiet surprised her. She went to Teddy's room. The map was rolled into a loose cylinder held in shape with paper clips. She peered down into the tube and saw colors and black, firm lettering of strange names that meant nothing to her. She was not a traveler. She would learn the names soon enough.

In the Sunday twilight she played a game with herself of trying to guess whether her son or her husband would be the first to return to her. It could be Teddy, because they had a rule that he was to be home before dark, and it could be Stephen, because the Merrillville show was over and he might want to hurry back and surprise his wife and son by his presence in the daylight.

She poured ginger ale into a glass. She sat in Stephen's chair with her legs curled under her, just holding the glass and watching the light become useless for painting.

It was Teddy. She'd guessed right. He came into the house whistling. His knees were shocked with green. A bruise smudged the corner of his left eye.

"What happened to you?" Fran asked.

"I played football."

"But it's not dark yet."

"Real football," Teddy said. "He's not home yet, huh?"

"It's a long way from Merrillville. He may not get here until after ten."

Teddy stole a mouthful of her ginger ale.

"Some of the guys wanted to copy my map," he said.

"I hope you told them to buzz off."

"Sure," he said. They had not come empty-handed to him, however. One friend offered math answers, which were always valuable. Another promised pictures of girls without clothes.

"Don't let other people get you to do their work for them," Fran warned.

He made an exasperated face at her and reached for her ginger ale again, but she tapped his hand. "Get your own," she said.

Some minutes before ten, Teddy came into the living room and announced, "Here he is."

"Goody," Fran said.

They met Stephen at the door. "The art pimp is home," he said.

"Don't say that," Fran scolded. She followed him into the kitchen with her hands on his shoulders. He felt she was steering him; he was pliable—happy to be home.

"I'm going to sleep until five tomorrow afternoon," he said. His wife put ice and water into a glass for him.

"How was the show, Dad?"

"The show was a success, Teddy." He gulped half the water. His son looked so awkward and mussed. He did so many things out of his sight; Stephen had no idea how to approach him. "Mom says you're having trouble in school."

Teddy looked at the floor. "A little," he said.

"But nothing you can't work your way out of?"

"I'll be OK," Teddy said.

"You've got to apply yourself." He finished the water. He rattled the cubes.

"Show us your map," Fran said.

"It's not done," Teddy replied.

"You told me it was done. I wouldn't have let you go out if I knew it wasn't done."

"It's *done*," Teddy said. "It just needs some finishing touches."

"Let's see it," his father said.

"OK. But it's not done."

Teddy left, and Stephen grabbed his wife and kissed her neck. Fran twitched away, laughing.

"We've got to get together and discuss art tonight," Stephen said. "If you know what I mean."

She laughed. "I know what you mean. What happened to the horizontal sword-swallower?"

He was about to tell her, but Teddy came into the room with his map. Stephen followed him to the kitchen table and watched as Teddy unrolled the heavy paper and weighted its corners.

"Why, Teddy, it's absolutely beautiful," Fran said. "It looks professional."

"Thanks," Teddy said softly.

Stephen did not know what to say. He had not expected the map to be so good.

Teddy waited, his eyes not on the map but on his father's bowed head. When his dad was away for any length of time, Teddy had to place him again in his mind. He had to pin him down and fit him back into the family. It was sometimes difficult.

"Is Moscow supposed to be so far west?" Stephen asked.

"Yes," Teddy said.

"I always pictured it more toward Siberia," Stephen said, lifting his eyes.

"No."

Stephen again turned his attention to the map. He couldn't get over how good it was. "It's really great, Teddy," he said. "It's Russia."

"Thank you."

"Although no one calls it Russia anymore," Stephen added. "It's the Soviet Union."

"*He* drew Russia," Fran said, slapping her husband's shoulder.

"Just a small point. It's quite fine work, Teddy."

"Thank you," Teddy said. He unburdened the corners and

the map snapped into its cylindrical shape, like a window shade going up.

"It's really amazingly good," his father said. "Are you sure that's how you spell Vladivostok?"

"Yes," Teddy replied, without consulting the map.

"You told us it wasn't finished," Stephen said. "It looks finished to me."

"That's because you didn't draw it," Teddy said.

A Night in the Garden

On the first day of the strike the men and women on the picket line were charged with a defiant enthusiasm. They slapped with their signs at the company's red trucks and created chants like college fight-songs to give voice and cadence to their grievances. The time was late October, and the weather was crisp and obliging. By the third day, the strikers had been through one round of picket duty. Rain had fallen most of the second day. No talks were scheduled between labor and management. TV news was losing interest.

Moss, the captain of Picket Team D, arrived in the rain on the strike's fourth day for the 4:00–8:00 a.m. shift. He had blisters on his big and little toes, the result of poor shoe and sock selection the first day of the strike, when he had zealously put in twelve hours on the line. He was thirty-three, unmarried, and so far had rather enjoyed the time off. The street was empty at four o'clock. Moss was the only person picketing until twenty minutes past the hour, when a woman carrying her sign arrived and began to picket several paces in front of him. She coughed, yawned, walked with her head bowed. Rain rolled off her slicker. Moss knew her name was Royster, because he had had to ask her when he took attendance the first time Team D picketed. She had spelled it for him without being asked.

They walked a narrow oval, seeking to remain as long as possible beneath the canopied entryway of the office's front door, where heat lamps had been installed so that people having business with the company might wait for cabs or limousines in comfort. The security guard stationed at the desk inside the front lobby had orders to keep the strikers moving if they tried to loiter where it was bright and warm.

So they marched slowly beneath the canopy and then back out into the rain, which intensified at around 5:00 a.m. At each end of the oval, after the woman turned, she and Moss passed each other like strangers. She never met his eyes. He didn't say a word. Moss could smell her perfume. The scent began to collect in the warm pocket beneath the canopy, and as the morning progressed the smell accrued. It was a very floral perfume, almost old-fashioned in its aggressiveness. Moss wasn't sure he liked it. He could not catch the scent of the perfume in the rain.

Toward seven o'clock four more pickets arrived, and Moss, as captain, had to chastise them for being late. Each was ready with an excuse, which Moss patiently listened to, but with a twist to his mouth which conveyed his skepticism. He had been able to get there at four. He supposed if he were going to be fair he should have spoken to Royster about being twenty minutes late. But at the time, in the rain and in the darkness, she had given the impression of having made an effort to get there on time.

Strike pay of a hundred dollars was issued to each person on the ninth day of the strike. Some joked about the amount. Others complained. That day, an egg was thrown at a company truck, leaving a pretty yellow star running down the truck's red door.

Team D had the 4:00–8:00 p.m. shift on that chilly afternoon. It was a pleasant, convenient time to picket, yet more than half the team was missing. One woman, whose husband was a lawyer, had said to Moss, "Call me when this is over. I've got better things to do." Now seven pickets marched. Moss was the only one with perfect attendance—the only one who had not missed a minute of picket duty. Snow could start falling at any time; the weather was cold enough. A good winter storm would chop any remaining enthusiasm down to nothing. Would Royster still picket if it snowed? Moss didn't know if *he* would, actually. Leave a picket sign stuck in a drift—that would be sufficient.

They moved in the same loose oval. Under the canopy warmth and light, then out again. Royster wore the same perfume; obvious, not unpleasant but edging up on being unpleasant. Moss's first thought had been to compliment her on her perfume, but he didn't want to lie to her. He could not make up his mind whether he liked her perfume or not. It seemed to him that a less liberal application might be more enticing. But he couldn't tell her such a thing. Maybe later, when they were friends, or lovers, or married, he could tell her that. When she loved him and valued his opinion; when she wanted to make him happy. But not now.

Three days later Team D had the 4:00–8:00 a.m. shift, and Moss was alone again. The security guard allowed him to walk his one-man oval within the boundaries of the canopy light. At five o'clock Royster arrived, and apologized for being late.

He was disappointed to see her. He thought she finally had wised up like all the others and stayed home in bed. He also had enjoyed feeling he was the only one with any defiance remaining, and then she appeared. She extended the reach of the oval he had walked. She stretched the turns outside the box of warm light he had enjoyed, forcing him into the cold and the dark.

It was later that morning that Moss informed her that he

liked her perfume. Not a lie, but not the absolute truth, either. Merely an excuse to talk to her. She looked startled; they hadn't spoken a word in an hour.

"What is it called?" Moss asked.

" 'A Night in the Garden.' "

He liked the name but was left with no openings. He might make a remark equating garden with flowers, but that would bring him too close to his objections to the overwhelming floral base of the scent, and so he said no more.

They moved through the turn of the oval together. "How are you holding up?" he asked.

"Just fine, Coach."

"I didn't mean . . . I mean, I had blisters for a while. And a sore throat. I'm always tired."

"Physical pains," she said. "I get charley horses here"—she touched the back of her knee. "I caught a cold picketing in the rain."

"Don't think I don't appreciate it," Moss said. "I wish everyone were as reliable as you."

"Give me their strike pay, then," she said. "I need the money."

"I can lend you some. I can lend you ten."

"Forget it. I've heard we're close to settling."

Moss had heard nothing of the sort. No negotiations were scheduled. Rumors abounded of scabs filling the jobs of strikers. "I wish I had your optimism," he said.

"We'll be back to work in no time," Royster said. "I *feel* it."

The strike was in its twentieth day when the company's owner, a man named Griffin, tried to walk through the picket line on his way to his limousine. He was struck in the head with an egg. A sharp crack, an explosion of yolk and shell, and the man went down to his knees. The yellow mess ran off the side of his face and onto his coat. Startled pickets rushed forward with offers of handkerchiefs, but the owner's aides rebuked them with curses and pulled the owner into the limousine, which sped off. In all the hubbub, the thrower of the egg remained at large.

On another early-morning shift a few days later, Moss was alone beneath the warm canopy when snow came whipping into the light. Royster arrived sometime after five.

"I'm here," she announced. "Check my name off your list."

"You're late," Moss said. "I can be on time. Why can't you?"

"I'm here, at least. Now check off my name."

"I will."

"Do it where I can see you."

"I left the list at home," Moss said. "Not so many people picket on this shift that I can't remember them when I get home."

"You're lucky I came at all," she fumed. "How dare you badger me for being a little late!"

"Carrying any eggs today?"

She grinned slyly. "You saw, huh?"

"I saw." Moss nodded. "Both eggings have been on our shift. You don't think somebody'll put two and two together?"

"Hey—Griffin was lucky it wasn't a rock," she said. "Next time, maybe it will be."

"What does that solve? You only succeeded in making the owner mad at the rank-and-file."

"Maybe not mad at," she said. "Maybe scared of."

"This is Day 24. And no talks are scheduled."

"It will end soon," she said firmly.

"All this optimism."

"We are hurting them where it counts," she said. "I know for a fact they are losing money because of a sympathetic backlash over this strike." She took her hand out of her pocket. An egg lay in her palm. "I carry one every time I picket," she said. "It's to remind me this isn't a walk in the park. I get so angry at them—and I'm glad to have it to throw."

"Why did you throw it at Griffin?" he asked.

She put the egg back. "Because he was such an unexpected

bonanza, for one," she said. "The owner! Right there in front of me. Could I let him get away? No! With his limo, his silver hair, his fancy clothes. And his attitude," she snarled. "He thought he could come right through us like we didn't exist. He was arrogant and insensitive. He *mocked* us."

"He said he just forgot and asked his driver to meet him at the wrong exit," Moss said.

"I don't believe that," she said. "All his flunkies—did they forget, too? But don't you see? He's saying our strike isn't important enough to remember. Even his explanation mocks us."

Later, she said, "That ten you offered? Is it still available?"

He gave her the money.

"I live with my mom," she explained. "She needs some things. Bread. Milk. Cough syrup."

"Eggs?" he said. She did not find his remark humorous.

He was forced to borrow three dollars from a friend coming on the 8:00 a.m.–noon picket shift in order to get his car out of the parking garage, and then he had to scrape through the litter in the glove compartment to find toll money.

Lending the ten, borrowing the three, and digging for change set in motion the first uneasy realization that his money was tight. He had bills that suddenly were going to be hard to pay. His savings suddenly appeared meager.

Royster asked again for money on the strike's thirtieth day. It was very cold and dry. Team D marched from eight to midnight, and the city around them was abundant and rich with the pre-holiday spirit.

"I can spare two dollars," Moss said. "But I have to pay parking and tolls. I had to borrow from a guy after I lent you that ten."

"I'm sorry," she said crossly. "But I *can* use the two dollars. And I *am* keeping track."

"How's your mom?" he asked.

"She worries—complains," Royster said. "She doesn't understand why anyone with a good job would ever strike. When I was a kid—fifteen—my dad was on strike for 301 days. Can you imagine? My mom has never recovered from that. I tell her we're going to settle soon, but she doesn't believe me."

"I don't either," Moss said. He was more and more impressed by the strategy of management. They had been shrewd to force a strike in late autumn, when any protracted walkout would run into the holidays.

"They're toying with us," Royster claimed bitterly, when she and Moss were alone before dawn on the thirty-fourth day. "They're toying with our most basic emotions. Christmas. Well-being. Providing for our families."

"It's a tool," Moss said. He had phoned his parents the previous evening to inform them he would not be visiting at Christmas. They offered to pay for his plane ticket, but he said he couldn't accept, because he had to picket. His mother had begun to cry. He hung up—worried about the bill, cutting the connection too abruptly to be fair to the disappointment he had implanted.

His desk at work was next to a window that overlooked the river. The river changed color with the weather—gray in the wind, slime-green in summer rains, cobalt-blue when ice was forming. Two days earlier he had stood on the riverbank opposite the office and found his window by counting up and over, and by identifying landmarks such as an antique coat tree, a terrarium on the sill, a cactus. A woman was working at his desk. He wanted to call her, ask her her name, learn what he could about her. Call her a scab. But he did nothing but begin to worry.

He told Royster what he had seen.

"Maybe she picked your desk for the view," she said breezily. "It probably has nothing to do with individuals."

Moss smiled uneasily. "I'm afraid I've been replaced," he said.

Part of the money he had put aside for his parents' Christmas presents went toward the electric bill, but he took what remained and went shopping. He felt like an impostor in the greedy crowds that filled the stores. Bumped off stride going through a revolving door, he lost a glove in the first store he entered and could not seem to regain his balance for the remainder of his shopping trip. He missed the orderliness of the picket oval.

For his father he bought a heavy brass horseshoe with mounting tacks and a leather-bound pocket French/English dictionary; his father didn't speak French but was always threatening to learn. For his mother he selected a box of bath powders in crisp little envelopes, scented floating candles, and a book on the history of crime fiction. For the two of them he sent a framed photograph taken of him the previous summer on a friend's boat. He was tanned, laughing, and full of life in the picture.

He wrapped the gifts in the previous Sunday's color comics, put them all in a large box with a brandied fruitcake, and then sealed the box and sent it off.

In the store where he bought his mother's bath powders, he had come upon a display of Royster's perfume. Several perfume and cologne bottles of various sizes containing the clear gold liquid revolved slowly on a blue velvet turntable. He decided to buy the largest bottle of cologne. He opened it, and she was there; he even looked behind him.

Royster was embarrassed when, on the forty-sixth day, he presented the package, his picket sign leaning against his leg.

"Take it," he said. He could smell it on her. She put the package in her shoulder bag.

"That was very nice," she said briskly. "You shouldn't have, though. I didn't get you anything."

"You're welcome."

She made a fist and banged her forehead. "I'm so thought-less! I *should* have brought you something. You've helped me. You've lent me money."

He picked up his sign with his gloved hand and continued to picket. She walked beside him.

"I've got to warn you," she said. "This is the last time I can picket from four to eight in the morning. Don't be upset."

"Why?" he asked.

She leaned close, though they were alone, and whispered, "For Christmas, I'm giving my mom the end of the strike. I'm telling her we settled. So if I'm working I don't have to be anywhere at four in the morning, right?"

"Will she believe you?" Moss asked.

"She believes whatever I tell her. She's like a little kid," Royster said. She cleared her throat. "I'm tired of her worrying so much. This will be a big relief for both of us."

"What will you do during the time she thinks you're at work?" he asked.

"Picket. Read. Window-shop. I'm looking forward to it." She tapped her bag. "Maybe you and me can meet somewhere and we'll have a drink of this. We can toast to a settlement before my birthday—which is in June, if you want to start planning what to buy me."

"That's perfume," Moss said.

"Perfume?"

"I got your brand. Your scent."

"You did?"

" 'A Night in the Garden.' "

"How'd you know that?"

"You told me once," Moss said.

They turned at the end of the oval.

She said, "Back then, did you ever tell me your name?"

The Jinx

The time is four-thirty on a cold Monday morning and the men of the Ultra Scavenger Service await the week's assignments of trucks and crews. Monday is the day Dooster, the foreman, must select a partner for Sweet, the Ultra jinx. Each truck has a driver, and two men called "tail gunners" who ride on small footholds at the rear of the truck and load the garbage into the compactor. These men engage in exhausting and dangerous work, and being paired with a jinx makes them understandably nervous.

Dooster begins to call out names. Everyone listens, smokes, coughs into his gloves. No one leaves, even after his name is called. Sweet himself leans patiently against the plate-glass window at the front of the room. He is not unaware of his station at Ultra, but he needs the money too much to quit and release everyone from the danger of working with him.

"You have your assignments," Dooster says to the men who still pack the room. But they have not heard the jinx's name called. "What . . . are you scared of the cold?" the foreman says.

One man pops out the door to the yard and his departure is like a cork being forced: drivers and tail gunners follow almost in a gush.

Dooster takes a moment, then announces the last crews. "Lupkin and Hayes with Reed on 24. Singh and Sweet with Cribones on 11."

And with that, the foreman's cup of coffee spills almost of its own volition.

Word passes in an instant among the men of Ultra that the jinx and Singh have been put together. Most agree this is a stroke of genius by Dooster. Nobody likes Singh because he is so obviously a foreigner. He wears a turban and a scraggly black beard, and has a high-pitched, unfamiliar voice. But he has endeared himself to his fellow workers by being easy for them to look down on. He and the jinx make a perfect couple. An upbeat mood infects the men of Ultra as they begin their day's work.

When Sweet awoke for work that morning at three-thirty, Rachel was still studying. He cleared a space at the kitchen table amid her books and papers, in order that he could eat his breakfast alongside her. She was tapping numbers into a calculator and humming. She kissed him and told him he possessed an unpleasant odor. Then she yawned.

Rachel was Sweet's age, and hard on the trail of a master's degree in Actuarial Sciences. Sweet had a bachelor's in History and was the Ultra Scavenger Service jinx. They had been married less than a year.

Sweet had gone to work at Ultra strictly for the money, rising well before dawn to apply for the job, and being turned down the first three times he tried because no one was absent those mornings. But on his fourth attempt, a Monday, two men did not appear, and Sweet became a tail gunner. The season was summer, tropically hot and damp.

On Sweet's first day, his partner, Stuckman, was lifting a bundle of newspapers when the dirty tin binding strap sliced surgically through his glove, then nearly through his thumb. He wanted to finish the route but his glove fingers kept filling with blood. Like test tubes, Sweet told Rachel.

Sweet was regarded suspiciously by the men of Ultra when they heard the story. Fourteen stitches were required to close Stuckman's wound, but he reported that thirteen had been taken. Something already in motion was given impetus by that mis-statement.

A certain wariness attended the following morning's announcement of Stuckman's replacement. Becker, also new on the job, with a month's seniority over Sweet, was given the assignment. The others approved of this pairing. They sensed something important taking place around them, a threat to the prevailing order, and they appreciated having a new man to test their suspicions and theories on.

The trucks and crews went out on another hot day. Sweet and Becker did not say much to each other but harbored their energy for the work, which went uneventfully until the next-to-last stop of the day. There, a customer was discarding an old lawn-mower. Becker, looking for a bargain, yanked the starter cord to see if the mower was worth salvaging. The engine did not start but the blade made one revolution and neatly sheared off the little toe on Becker's left foot. A call was put in to the dispatcher for an ambulance, and the men of Ultra heard the truck number and the nature of the emergency and looked very uneasily at one another.

Sweet, Singh, and Cribones are working through a neighborhood on the north side of town. Lunchtime is approaching, and Cribones has maintained a pace that will deliver them at the appointed hour to a convenience store where a girl he has dated works. She gives him free ham-salad sandwiches and coffee. Cribones's tail gunners don't disrupt his plans, which is all he asks of them. He knows Sweet's reputation, but he feels safe in the cab, behind the wheel, thinking about lunch.

The ambulance took Becker away, his toe riding along in a baggie of shaved ice, and Sweet and the driver made the route's last stop, emptied the truck at the landfill, then returned to the yard. Sweet was eager to provide his version of the incident but no one wanted to hear it. The men of Ultra had not heard even Becker's side of the story, but they had heard enough: a man had lost a toe while working with Sweet, one day after a man nearly lost a thumb working with Sweet.

Sweet was kept in the garage the next day. Dooster explained that they had an odd number of tail gunners, and on such an occasion somebody was held back to work around the yard. Sweet got the idea when he saw a truck go out with three men on the back. He spent the day hosing down the repair bays, washing the windshields on the idle trucks, filling the pop machine, and pulling weeds along the fence that surrounded the yard.

Later, he cornered the foreman. "Why aren't I on a truck today?"

"I told you. Odd number of gunners. Low man has to stay behind and do the menials."

"One truck had three guys on it, I noticed."

"A special route," Dooster said. He would not meet Sweet's eye. "Something new we're trying."

"Not very cost-efficient."

"We'll see, won't we?"

"Tell me the truth. Nobody wanted to work with me, right?"

"Did I say that?"

"I didn't cut off Becker's toe. I didn't slice Stuckman's thumb."

"You were there, though," Dooster said. "Two bad accidents your first two days on the job. That makes these men very nervous. They know they're never going to make a living with their brains, sitting in a nice safe office, so they become much more conscious of their body's condition. They're like athletes, Sweet. They see Becker go down for two, three months at least, and Stuckman out a couple weeks. It scares them. They look for someone to blame."

"That's absurd," Sweet said.

"Sure it is. Maybe," the foreman said. "Tomorrow I'll put you on a truck with someone. But these men don't like to change their minds. I want you to know that."

Sweet went home and his wife was in the shower washing her hair. She finished, held out a hand, and hooked the towel Sweet tossed.

"Open the window," Rachel said. She was rosy and a little out of breath. "God, you stink! You smell like something crawled inside your shirt and died."

"They think I'm a jinx. Nobody will work with me."

"What a silly thing to say," she said, laughing. "From what you told me, you had nothing to do with those men getting hurt."

"I *didn't*. But I was there, I'm new, so I must be guilty," Sweet said. "The foreman told me the others are like athletes— they make a living with their bodies."

"*Athletes?*" Rachel scoffed. "Athletes choose to be what they are. Would these guys be garbagemen if they had the smarts to be anything else?"

"No," Sweet said. "But they understand that. They know they'll never be anything else—so it's vital to them that they stay in one piece. A jinx scares them witless."

"Witless is the word exactly," she said. "Don't take it so seriously. You aren't one of them. You know you'll move on before too long."

"But I want them to be able to count on me," Sweet said.

"Can I count on you to burn those clothes?"

He watched his wife wrap herself in the towel and step from

the tub. He was conducting a test of his own there in the damp, slippery bathroom, to see if he had also become a jinx in his own home. But Rachel moved deftly across the slick tile and into their bedroom, although when she sat down to study while combing the knots from her hair she cut her finger on the sharp edge of a page. Sweet did not hear her cry out because he was already in the shower, and Rachel did not make the connection.

Sweet and Singh are eating lunch in the convenience store, leaning against a frozen-food cooler at the rear. They must eat there because Cribones is using the truck's warm cab to entertain his girlfriend, who did indeed have three free ham-salad sandwiches and a large black coffee waiting for him. The driver dropped Sweet and Singh at the store, and picked up the girl and the food. Cribones told his tail gunners he would retrieve them in a half-hour.

Sweet buys a newspaper and reads while he eats his sandwich. He is angry, because he has been on his feet all morning, and must now remain standing through lunch. Singh touches Sweet's arm and asks, "May I read the financial section, please?"

An hour passes before Cribones returns. The girl jumps down out of the cab wearing Cribones's hat, and he has to yell after her to bring it back. She teases him, twirling the hat on a finger, daring him to come for it. Sweet snatches the hat from her on his way to the truck and angrily wings it in at the smirking driver.

Sweet and Singh take their places on the tail but the truck does not move for nearly five minutes, and when it finally does, Cribones ignores the remainder of the route and returns with undue speed and gnashing of gears to the garage. The driver immediately goes into a conference with Dooster, and when the meeting is finished Cribones goes to Sweet and loudly declares, "You are bad luck *in person*."

. . .

Dooster kept his promise and put Sweet back on a truck. By rotating the jinx through the roster of gunners and drivers, he kept complaints to a minimum. Working with Sweet became a trial to be weathered, like a bout with the flu. Rachel's summer session ended, but her new semester began just after Labor Day, and with their schedules Sweet sometimes would not speak to her for two or three days at a time. She would be only a muttering in the next room while he slept, or a dark shape in bed when he left for work at a quarter after four in the morning.

The foreman takes Sweet aside after the trucks are put away and the men either have gone home or are horsing around in the yard.

"What happened today? At lunch?" Dooster asks.

"I don't know. What happened?"

"I couldn't reach Cribones on the radio for nearly an hour. He's kinda vague as to why."

"That's between you and him, then."

"Was he with a girl?"

"Take it up with him," Sweet says.

"I did. He won't admit to anything. He's been caught before with his radio off. We've found evidence he's had girls in his cab, which is automatic dismissal. I'm putting him back on the tail for a month," Dooster says.

"He no doubt blames me."

"You can count on that."

Cribones is waiting for Sweet when he comes into the yard. A few men are still around, talking, smoking, laughing.

"What'd you tell him?" Cribones asks sullenly.

"Nothing."

"I don't believe you."

Sweet shrugs. He is exhausted and cold.

"I've gotta ride the tail for thirty days because of you," Cribones says.

"I didn't turn off the radio. I didn't turn it off the other time you got caught, either."

"You *did* talk about me!"

"He asked questions that were none of my business," Sweet says. "I didn't answer them."

"When are you going to quit here?"

"I need the money," Sweet says. "I have to put my wife through school."

"Are you bad luck for her, too?" Cribones asks.

"You'd have to ask her."

A block away he is crossing the street when Singh pedals by on a bicycle. He waves and gives the handlebar bell a jingle. Sweet wonders where he came from. He watches him until he is out of sight, and all the time he watches he expects Singh to fall off the bike, to snag a chain, to snag his unraveling turban in the spokes and break his neck.

Rachel is studying when he gets home. The book she reads from is *Theories of Life Expectancy*. He sniffs himself surreptitiously for that dead smell she sometimes accuses him of possessing.

She asks, looking up at him, "Why no kiss?"

"You'll say I stink."

"Do you?"

"I don't know."

"Kiss me," she says, with an impatient tapping of her pencil against her palm. He kisses her lips. She presses a hand to his chest, he feels the faint prick of the pencil point through his shirt. He steps back and she tests the air with a series of delicate sniffs; she samples his taste by running her tongue lightly over her mouth.

"Not bad," she says. "Not *fragrant*, but I know you work hard. Did I ever tell you I once followed you for a block when you were working near school? You were so fixated on that garbage. Lift the cans, empty them, ride to the next stop. Lift, empty, ride. Lift, empty, ride. I don't know if I'd do the same to put you through school. I loved you for doing it for me."

"They asked me at work if I brought you bad luck, too," Sweet says.

Rachel grimaces. "Still the jinx, huh?"

"Do I?"

"I *am* a little blue. I don't feel so hot," she says. "Did you cause that?"

"Don't feel so hot how?"

"Random pains. I'm smoking off and on again."

"I know. I smelled it," Sweet says. "If you smoke—and spend time with the jinx—you're sure to get cancer."

"Well, I don't spend time with you—so I'm safe, aren't I?" she says.

He hangs his work clothes on a nail driven into the wall outside the back door, and arranges his boots there on the floor. Rachel follows him into the kitchen, carrying the pencil, keeping a beat against her palm.

"Can you handle some bad news?" she asks. And before he can answer yes or no, she says, "Tuition's going up."

"How much?"

"Twelve percent."

"When did you hear this?" Sweet asks. He does not bother to compute the new figure; the school will do that for him. He asks questions of Rachel as a way to bleed off the anger and frustration that fill him.

"A while ago," she says. "I didn't want to tell you because we were having a tough time."

"Is there a *good* time to hear about a tuition increase?" Sweet asks.

"Well, now I've told you," she says. She nibbles the end of the pencil. "I've been feeling pretty alone lately. I imagine you have, too."

"It's just the hours we keep," Sweet says.

"And in forty years we'll laugh about this?"

. . .

The following morning, Sweet is paired with Cribones. They go out into the cold, and the day is exhausting for Sweet, because Cribones sulks about being a tail gunner at all and doesn't do his share. Sweet, having heard Rachel's assessment of his job, also thinks too much about what he is doing, and the hazed rhythm of the work eludes him.

At lunch, Cribones says, "I asked to be paired with you. Nobody could believe it."

"I'm honored."

"But I'm smarter than they think. I want you to do to me what you did to Becker."

"I didn't do anything to Becker," Sweet says.

"You did something," Cribones says. "He's getting paid what we make to sit home and watch TV. Now, I'm not willing to give up a toe—but I'll take a bad sprained ankle if it means I can sit out this suspension. This here is too much like work."

"I can't help you," Sweet says.

"Sure you can. You're a jinx."

"I am not a jinx."

"You *are*, though. Just work your old black magic on me. I'll gladly limp home."

"No," Sweet says.

"I'll pay you."

Sweet does not reply. He merely listens.

"How about twenty-five dollars for each week of disability?"

"Fifty," Sweet says. "For fifty dollars a week, I'll see what I can do."

The Fire

Two boys carrying men's magazines ran down a path through the woods. They thought they were being followed. Wind raised by their haste fluttered the magazines open in a shuffling of startling pictures. The magazines were stolen. The boys were named Mitch, who was ten years old, and Donald, who was within a month of nine.

Donald was the faster runner, though, and he beat Mitch to a creek which in that hot summer had pulled in its borders to the width of a rope, and he led him over the flat stones, then up the bank on the other side.

Mitch looked back and fell, spilling his magazines. He gathered them on his knees. Donald watched the woods. The only movement was the twitch of leaves they'd stirred in passing. Donald felt they had gotten away. Mitch was sure they were being followed. They went up a long hill that in the winter was a sled run.

At the top of the hill was an abandoned water pump and Mitch had worked a board loose in its wooden base. The cavern beneath smelled of minerals, and damp, mildewed paper. The two boys each chose two magazines for closer inspection, and hid the rest beneath the pump.

The pump was out in the open, in the sunshine, but Mitch and Donald retreated to the shadows at the edge of the woods. It was cooler there, and safer. Their breathing settled. The magazines had names like *Sir*, *Gent*, *Rogue*, and *Mister*. Mitch had discovered an abundance of them in a garage he passed every day on his way to meet Donald in the woods. There were so many magazines that they covered one wall several stacks deep, with the stacks reaching nearly to the ceiling, and one of these towers fell over like a tree, hitting the floor with an echoing *poom!* Mitch and Donald scurried the twenty steps from the garage to the woods. Both carried a stack of magazines held out in front of them like bombs.

Little was said as they gravely studied the pictures. Perhaps only "Look at this," or something whispered. Donald had seen his mother undressed on occasion, but he could not make sense of the women in the magazines, or the awkward poses they assumed. The expressions on their faces were especially perplexing. Some seemed to be sharing a joke with someone. Others, their mouths open, appeared startled.

In time they had looked at every stolen magazine and hidden them all beneath the pump. Mitch put the board back in place. He drew the pump handle up, which set the machinery to clanking and reverberating deep in the ground. But no water rose. The spout had a wart at the end to hold a bucket.

"My dad told me this used to give water," Mitch said.

Beyond the pump was a wide field of tall, dry grass, some trees, and, about two football fields away, a blacktopped road. The field continued on the other side of the road, ending at a row of houses; Donald's house was in that row. Mitch lived in the opposite direction, down the hill, beyond the woods.

They had made up a telephone code. One called the other, let the phone ring once, then hung up. It was a way for one to alert the other that he was going to be at the pump. The other could come or not. Usually they met. It was a way to cut the distance they had to travel, and for Mitch to avoid Donald's parents, who didn't like him.

Mitch took off his baseball cap. He pulled up the edge of his T-shirt and wiped his face. His hair was damp, with a trench circling his head where the cap had squeezed. Both boys had necklaces of dirt in the creases in their necks.

Donald stretched out on his back in the shade with his eyes closed and chewed on a moist end of grass.

"Let's get a drink from the creek," Mitch said.

"My mom'll make us some lemonade," Donald replied, not opening his eyes.

"I want to stay in the woods."

Donald heard Mitch move away down the hill. Donald rolled over, got to his hands and knees, stood up. He followed his friend.

Low places in the creek bed held the last green pools of water. This water had a scummy, dangerous look that repelled Donald, but didn't seem to bother Mitch. He lightly fanned aside the surface algae, then took three quick swallows from the dark water he had cleared. Pills of algae stuck to his lips. He grimaced and spat them away.

"Good?" Donald asked sarcastically.

Mitch stood up. He seemed oldest to Donald when he was willing to try something that Donald was not.

"Yum!" Mitch said, rubbing his stomach, and spitting some more.

For a while they roamed up and down the creek looking for snakes, but none were out. They went back up the hill. Donald lay down again. Mitch worked on the pump some more. He put his ear to the spout to listen for the rumble of rising water, but there was nothing but the diminishing echo of the pump machinery.

"Let's go to my house," Donald said.

"I want to stay here."

Donald shrugged. "I'm going. There's nothing to do here." He started to walk away, and he didn't bother to see if Mitch was going to follow. Donald couldn't see his house from the pump, but he could see the flag his family flew in the back yard. When the sun hit the pole right it sparkled like a silver rod. His sister frequently could be found circling it, pretending she was a horse.

Donald heard the dry rush of grass as Mitch came after him. He bounded across the field like a plains animal, rising up and settling back in his stride, running with the fervor of prey. He caught Donald a good hundred yards from the road.

"Let's *do* something," Mitch pleaded, his breathing quick.

"OK. What?"

As if he had known all along, Mitch took a book of matches from his pocket. Without a word the two boys turned back toward the pump and walked to it and then past it, finally kneeling down together in the shadows.

"Where'd you get them?"

"My mom's purse," Mitch said. The matches had scarlet heads, with glints of phosphorus. Mitch tore out a match, closed the cover, then struck the match and set fire to a stalk of grass. It heated orange, looking lit from within, then cooled, blackened, curled, and broke apart. Smoke floated through Donald's hair; he was crazy about the smell of smoke.

"Let me do one," he said. He was comfortable with matches. His parents let him burn the contents of the family's wastebaskets in an incinerator in their basement. Papers became spy documents set afire an instant before detection; milk cartons slowly combusted with people still trapped inside. And once—the best time he remembered—his father threw away an old pirate-ship lamp and Donald watched the leathery sails, the masts, and the hull consumed, the pirates leaping screaming from the flames into a sea of flames, and there was no saving them.

He struck a match and burned a stick. A dampness at its

core frustrated the fire. He wanted to try another, but Mitch had taken the matches and moved out of the shadows.

"If we only had a frog or snake," Mitch said dreamily. He snapped a match and flipped it away even as the head ignited. The air put the match out before it landed.

They were standing in grass up to their knees. Neither boy spoke of his desire to set fire to the field. It was like an exciting, shameful secret, the simple desire to set in motion and witness some form of destruction.

Mitch crouched over a clump of dry grass and dropped a burning match into the center of it, and Donald took the book ten feet away and lit his own stand. The smoke rose in a white column that mimicked the twist of the grass. Sparks jumped on the breeze and rode it a short distance, and where some touched down they died, but others flourished. Mitch's fire had begun to chase after Donald's fire, which was moving toward the road.

The pump had once been part of a farm that failed (for lack of a reliable supply of water, among other things), and three thick rolls of wire fencing had been left behind. They were stuffed with grass, home to mice and snakes. The fire spread far more rapidly than the boys had imagined possible; it rushed along almost merrily. But they would have had a chance to stamp the fire out if they had kept it away from those rolls of fencing, which made a full-throated *poof!* sound as they caught; the heat pushed Donald back.

Mitch ran to the pump. He worked the useless handle with such panicked zest that his feet left the ground on the updraft.

"Stop that!" Donald shouted. He gave Mitch a clean, hard punch to the chest. They never fought, and perhaps the blow caught him by surprise, but Mitch spun off the pump base and onto the dirt. He got to his feet, brushed himself off, and returned to the pump. He dislodged the loose board in the base and removed a copy of *Fur!* He replaced the board, then took the magazine to where the fire burned weakly and began to slap at it. The leading edge of the fire was a good hundred yards away; the roar of it was very clear.

Mitch tossed the *Fur!* aside and stood up. He calmly took hold of Donald by the shirt. "I don't know how this fire started," he said. "And neither do you."

He released Donald and ran away then, down the hill.

Donald followed a route home perpendicular to the path of the fire. He kept to the shadowed woods. He stopped and dried his eyes on his shirt. He was thirsty and he smelled of smoke. He reached the edge of the woods, crossed a thin strip of high grass, and stepped out onto the road. Tar pulled at his shoes when he walked. To his left the road vanished in the smoke. He was out in the open so he ran toward the fire like any other curious boy. He saw only thick smoke, but then the wind cleared a space for him and he saw that the fire had effortlessly jumped the road.

Donald heard a low moan, a siren. Something moved on the road, a flickering in the tar. He went closer and saw that it was a mouse. Its tail and ears were burned off, its skin charcoal paper. A snake slithered farther on, the tar tough going. A rabbit broke cover. Its spine looked to be on fire. Donald stopped; he began to walk backward.

A police car was progressing carefully down the road. The siren bubbled in the car's throat. Donald heard its tires, the hot, sucking sound they made, and jumped into the burning field; he didn't think he had been seen. Sparks blew through his hair.

His mother was on the roof of their house, wetting down the shingles with the garden hose. She wore sunglasses and smoked a cigarette. All up and down the row of houses women made their stands on their roofs with garden hoses, prepared to drain their wells to save their homes from a fire he had set on a lark of destruction. He had never expected his mother to be drawn into his mischief.

The houses were similar, each set on a quarter-acre lot, some of the back yards fenced, some with wash hung out, some with big plastic flowers pinwheeling in the wind like cheerful weather gauges. The heart of the fire was a good hundred yards away yet, but sent smoke and sparks and cinders ahead like the pounding before a hurricane.

Donald's house had the only flagpole. His mother wanted a fence to hold her children in, and to string wild roses through. Donald knew she would get the fence, in time.

"*Where* have *you* been?" his mother screamed. He looked up at her; a cool mist from the hose fell in his eyes. She stuck her cigarette into the stream, then dropped the butt into the gutter.

"Playing," he answered.

"Fire department's coming! Daddy's on his way home!"

Donald watched his mother take her cigarettes out of her shorts pocket and light one. He imagined her delaying her ascent to the roof until she was sure she had a fresh pack and matches. When the fire was close enough she would get lights off the swirling embers.

She looked acrobatic up there, young and daring; she seemed almost to be enjoying herself. She had been a gymnast in high school, then broke her ankle falling from the balance beam. She met Donald's father when her leg was in a cast. She teased that she hadn't been able to run away, or she would have. She looked at home on the roof, on the edge of her balance.

When cinders fell in the yard, Donald carefully ground them with his toe until they looked cold to the touch. He noticed that the bottoms of his jeans were full of tiny burn holes, as if chewed by moths. He undid the flagpole rope. The pulleys squeaked as he lowered the flag. His father had taught him one evening to fold the flag into its tricornered package, but now he just hugged the flag, with its smell of musty cloth and smoke, and hurried inside.

Soon his father arrived home. He rushed through the house carrying a red fire-extinguisher, and he didn't see his son, who sat in a corner of the family room sobbing into the flag. Donald remembered the brilliant whiteness of his father's shirt; and how his tie bounced against his chest as he ran through the room, the tie tack keeping the tie in place.

The roof of the Benson house, to the south, had caught fire. Mrs. Benson, her disbelieving face smeared with smoke and tears, helplessly watched a fire the size of her washing machine burn in the center of her roof. Her husband was on a sales trip to Ohio. She had no children. Donald's mother covered her ears when Mrs. Benson began to scream

The first fireman appeared then. Mrs. Benson fainted at the sight of him; she folded downward, her knees, held properly together, hitting the ground first, then her rump; then she unfolded out along the grass. The fireman dragged a thick, empty hose. Even after signaling for the water he had to wait several long moments for the pressure, while the fire ate at the Bensons' roof. A second fireman, running clumsily in his black rubber coat, boots, and heavy hat, joined him, and then the water filled the hose and jetted out, first onto the grass (a splash soaking Mrs. Benson's peaceful, unconscious face and reviving her), then up the wall, and finally to the fire on the roof.

Donald's father emptied his fire extinguisher on a stubborn flame burning at the rear property line. The ground was left cool and whitened like spat toothpaste. It also marked the fire's closest approach to the house. He kept glancing up at his wife on the roof. She had taken a seat, draping the hose across her lap and dangling her feet over the gutter. He had rolled up the sleeves of his shirt, careful to put his cuff links in his pocket, but he had not yet been extended in his efforts sufficiently to require loosening his tie.

Two more firemen pulling a hose appeared between two houses down the row. They were almost nonchalant. The Benson house was no longer burning. The first hose on the scene had already cut the fire down to manageable size. The fire was nothing out of the ordinary: a summer field-fire pushed by a moderate wind, the whole thing caught in time, the damage to the Benson house notwithstanding. Water came to the second hose. One of the firemen sang an Everly Brothers song.

In minutes it was over and Donald was sent across the street to retrieve his sister, sent to a neighbor for safekeeping. His father helped his mother down from the roof. In her excitement of climbing up there she had knocked over the ladder. They were laughing in the kitchen when their children returned. Donald's father went back to work. His mother changed clothes, then made lunch.

A downpour began that night, and Donald listened to hear the earth hissing as it cooled. The next morning he played with his sister where he could keep an eye on the field. Freshly scrubbed and painted a flat black, the field looked as if an utterly new and strange landscape had been laid on it during the night.

A week went by, during which time he did not see Mitch at all; this was unusual, because they were friends. The phone never rang its code calling him to their meeting place. Donald wondered if he would ever go to that spot again.

He thought he detected fresh green in the field but he was afraid to look closely. He wanted the grass to grow quick enough for the naked eye to discern; he wanted every trace of the fire hidden.

On a Saturday morning he took his seat at breakfast, and then his mother sent his sister out of the room. His father was drinking coffee. He hadn't shaved, which was his way of enjoying the weekend. His hand lay on an overturned magazine, the edges of which were lightly browned. A pair of Donald's jeans were hung over the back of a chair.

"Don," his father said, calling his son by a name they never used, "the fire department says they think you started the fire last week."

Donald's mother set a bowl of cereal in front of him. Yellow bean-shaped objects floated in the milk. He tried to remember what they were called. He wondered if a response to his father's declaration was required of him.

No, Donald said to himself.

His father picked up the blue jeans. He smoothed them across his lap.

Donald's father said, "The fire was started near that old pump where you play. They found a book of matches."

His father paused again. The kitchen was quiet except for the sounds of his mother cooking. His father was listing evidence, clues, like a detective, but he hadn't put the charge directly to Donald. He hadn't asked Donald if he had set the fire.

No, Donald said again to himself. No, he nearly said out loud.

"A policeman saw a boy run out of the woods," his father continued. "He had on blue jeans and a T-shirt. He looked scared—and ran into the field toward our house. They think he started the fire. Why else would he run? When I got home that day—the first time—you were sitting in the family room crying."

Donald took a swallow of water and for an instant he thought it had caught in his throat, he thought he was going to spray the table as a diversion from his fright. The police. The fire department. Taking the time to seek out the fire's point of origin. Gathering witnesses. Collecting clothes for examination. They put it all together and came to a conclusion: he was it.

No, Donald said again to himself. His eyes locked on his father until his father looked at him. Then he hid. He was scared to death, but he was prepared to lie.

"The Bensons' roof was badly damaged," his father said. "A lot of people were afraid their house—everything they owned—was going to burn up. That fire scared many, many people."

"Like *me*," his mother said, so harshly Donald flinched.

"*Our* house could've easily burned down," his father said.

"All your things—*gone. Everything* gone. People could've been killed. Animals *were* killed. All that land was burned."

Donald was careful not to look defiant, for fear his defiance would be challenged. He hardly listened to what his father said because it was all stuff he knew; he had scared himself for many nights thinking how close he had come to causing serious trouble. Trouble there was no talking his way out of. Trouble that went on and on.

But now he was alert for the question, and the question didn't come.

His mother took away the empty cereal bowl; he didn't recall eating, though he tasted mild and spongy sugar on his tongue. She refilled his water glass and he drank most of it.

"How did you burn your pants so badly?" his mother asked in her sharp voice. His father looked up at her and something in his eyes broke apart; she had jammed her hand into his delicate construction.

"I was here when the fire got here," Donald said. "Sparks must've hit my pants. They burned right through the flag, too." The flag was in his bedroom, wadded on a shelf in the closet. No one had mentioned replacing it.

His mother put a plate of eggs, bacon, and hash-browns in front of Donald. She set a glass of orange juice and a saucer of toast, butter, and jam next to it. The offering soothed Donald: he was not in such disfavor that they would stop feeding him. "Eat," his mother commanded.

His father turned over the magazine. He slid it across the table to Donald. "They found this near the pump," his father said.

It was the copy of *Fur!* Mitch had slapped at the fire with. The woman on the cover, a redhead with her tongue protruding, had been burned in half, from her navel down, with another perfect brown hole in the center of her forehead. The magazine smelled like its hiding place.

"Del Hodge's wife said she saw a boy she thought was you running out of their garage with an armload of this garbage," his father said.

Donald felt the case his father was making tightening around him. Witnesses were everywhere. His father might be on the verge of naming someone who had seen him set match to grass.

His blunders were all over the crime, but the question hadn't been asked of him and so he said nothing. His mother took the *Fur!*, put it in the wastebasket under the sink, then walked out of the kitchen. Donald's father sat back in his seat and drank his coffee. Everyone seemed to be taking a break. Donald ate his breakfast.

With the quiet, with a pause in the amassing of evidence, Donald felt at peace. He did not look at his father, who whispered very suddenly, "Don't you lie to your mother."

"I didn't."

"Don't!" His father finished his coffee. They both waited.

His mother returned with a basket of wash and went out back to hang it up. She held the wooden pins in her mouth. A wind popped the sheets, which gleamed like fresh grafts on the burned field. Donald and his father sat at the table watching her. She brought in the empty basket, the unused pins rolling in the bottom. She seemed surprised to see Donald still there.

"Did you want to say something?" she said.

"No," Donald said.

"You can go, then," she said, not looking at him.

"You don't play with Mitch much anymore," his father said.

"No," Donald said. He lingered at selected points along the route of his departure—the table edge, the sink to drop off his empty plate and glasses, the back door—so that he did not appear to be leaving with the haste he felt necessary. He expected them to call him back, to say his freedom was a tease and that they demanded he tell them the truth, and a part of him wanted to give them the opportunity to do so. But they let him go. He didn't know why.

Outside and out of their sight, he began to run over the blackened ground until he crossed that line where the fire had reached, and the field beyond was luxuriant, cool, and green. He slipped low through it, staying out of sight, and then he crossed the road and he was in the woods again. He didn't think he had been observed, but he couldn't be sure.

Black Bart

Black Bart's six-year-old son, Dale, helped his father pack the satchel for the last time that summer season. Into the satchel went Black Bart's black boots and black steel spurs, the black leather vest, the black silk kerchief, and then Black Bart went out to the back yard and removed his black shirt and black trousers from the clothes line. They were still damp. Through the summer the shirt and pants never dried, either being wet from his sweat at work or damp from washing and a night on the line in the dew.

Black Bart folded the shirt and trousers and placed them in the satchel. He handed Dale the six-shooters in their black leather holsters with the row of blanks on the belt, and the boy's proud, practiced hands wrapped them into a compact train-robber's bundle and set them atop the clothes. Black Bart took his black hat from its peg on the wall. He set it on his son's head and together they carried the satchel into the kitchen.

Black Bart's wife, Julie, was in the kitchen packing boxes. She had prepared a cup of coffee for her husband and a glass of milk and a piece of toast for her son. In her packing she would take a plate or a glass and wrap it in a sheet of newspaper and put it in the box; the boxes were saved from move to move. Out through the back door Black Bart could see that their eleven-year-old VW bus was nearly filled with their belongings. That evening, when Black Bart returned from work, he and Julie and Dale would drive to Ocutla, Florida, where a job as Sneaky Pete awaited.

"Jordan will pay you in cash, won't he?" Julie asked Black Bart.

"Yes. I've talked to his secretary and it's all arranged."

"In cash? It's got to be in cash. There won't be a place to cash a check that size when you get home. The bus needs oil and gas. Dale has to start school the day after tomorrow, so we should leave tonight."

Black Bart nodded patiently. His wife did the worrying in the family, gratefully taking on his share and his son's share as a sort of perverse reward; Black Bart's only responsibility was to be available on short notice to listen as she delineated their accumulated concerns.

Cube Jordan, Black Bart's boss, knew it was the final day of the season as well as, maybe better than, anyone else. He was creator and sole proprietor of Fort Fun and it was the nature of the men and women he hired that when Fort Fun closed its doors at the end of the season they were anxious to be on the road; and for that they needed cash. This all had been explained to Black Bart by Jordan's secretary, Brenda, a pretty, vacuous girl of twenty, and so Black Bart accepted it as the truth.

"This is the day you promised to take Dale to work with you," Julie said.

"It is?" Black Bart asked with feigned skepticism.

"Yes," she said. "You said you would take him on the last day of the season, and today is the last day."

Black Bart finished his coffee. He tipped the tin cup way

back to be sure he got it all. Then he abruptly slammed the cup down on the table so it bounced and spun on his finger like a six-shooter. Julie, and then Dale, began to laugh.

"All summer," she continued, "he's been a good boy and you said you'd take him—"

"And today is the last day," Black Bart said. Then he drew his upper lip slowly back from his teeth in a cruel snarl and picked at his teeth. "I gotta ride hard, Ma, and chillens only slow me down."

"You promised, Black Bart," Dale said.

"Get me my timepiece!" Black Bart ordered the boy.

Dale ran to his parents' bedroom in the back of the house. The four-room house they had rented for the season was almost empty. All the summer contents of the house had swirled in a state of disarray not unlike weightlessness, with no organization, no assigned place for anything but the man, the woman, and the child, who each belonged to the others.

"He has to pay in cash," Julie warned in a low voice.

"He will, honey," Black Bart said. "Hey, Joel and Angel are going to Ocutla. I could ask him if they want to travel together."

"Joel drives like a maniac," Julie said. "We'd never keep up."

Dale returned with Black Bart's watch, a durable, cheap brand without a wrist strap. He put it in his pocket.

"Can you ride and shoot?" he asked with a hard, probing gleam in his eye.

The boy nodded.

"I ain't got time nor room in my heart for greenhorns. I got to know right off—can I use you in my gang?"

"You bet," Dale said.

"You got a horse?"

Dale said he did.

"Let's go see her," Black Bart said. He got the satchel off the kitchen floor and followed Dale out to the back yard. The sun was warm and high. It was a Labor Day of perfect weather. Two old bicycles leaned against the fence. One was larger than the other. They came with the rented house.

"How long will it take you today?" Julie asked.

"A half-hour," Black Bart said. He put the satchel in the basket of the bigger bicycle.

"Be careful," Julie said. "Watch him." Black Bart nodded. He usually called her when he arrived at Fort Fun but they had had the phone taken out the day before.

"We will," he said, and kissed her goodbye.

Dale kissed his mother briefly on the cheek and then got a running start and bounded onto the smaller bike, pumping hard to get over the small rise out of the yard to the lane. When the lane met the highway they turned and waved again.

There were six hills between the house and Fort Fun. The first was the smallest, a dilapidated mailbox at the top to mark it, and Black Bart sailed over it no-handed. Dale, though, labored near the crown, becoming almost stationary in his effort, but then standing hard on the pedals and going over. The road between the hills was merciless in its denial of favors. If the hills had rolled one into the other there would have been a chance to build speed on the down sides. But fifty or sixty yards of flat country road separated the hills, and Black Bart took to circling back behind his son to see him safely over. Approaching the top of the second, third, and fourth hills, the boy had to get off and walk the bike.

"That is some worthless horse you got," Black Bart said as they went along the road toward the fifth hill. The boy wiped his face with his hand and would not look at his father.

"Whoa her up there a minute," Black Bart said.

Dale swung the bike to the side of the road and jumped off, letting it careen on into a ditch. Black Bart dismounted and jumped down by the fallen bike.

"Can you see it from there?" he asked his son.

"No," Dale said.

"Lend a hand, then," Black Bart said. They covered the bike with weeds.

"We should leave a sign," Dale said.

Black Bart smiled proudly. He had not thought of this. They found a large red rock and set it on the shoulder of the road by the hidden bicycle. Dale sat on the seat of Black Bart's bike; the satchel was in the front basket; Black Bart stood to pedal and so they went on their way.

"Hold tight," Black Bart warned, "this baby bucks."

Black Bart had stopped at the top of the sixth hill on the first day of the season and looked for a time down on Fort Fun, not thinking too much about the place, just happy to have the job. He considered himself an actor and the part of Black Bart was, he told Julie, "at least hard work," more testing of his stamina and patience than his talent, but at least a role. The job paid $222 a week (plus whatever he could wrangle in tips: virtually nothing, it turned out; people did not tip train robbers) and Black Bart saw that $222-a-week figure more than anything else when he looked for the first time down at Fort Fun sitting there like an old-timer with his hand out, a lopsided rectangle of high wood-post walls, a small-gauge railroad he would rob every thirty minutes, the stagecoach trails, the hotel, the jail, the concession stands, the souvenir booths, the green lawns that would be pounded nearly to dust by tourists and the summer heat, the entire enterprise sitting in the very center of a parking lot which at the height of the season would be a glittering, polychromic cookie sheet of baking automobiles.

But on the final day of the season Black Bart did not pause, even to spit, at the top of the hill. He and Dale coasted down the hill and through the gate to Fort Fun.

A group of Injuns, sunburned and paunchy after hitting their peak in early August, sat in the shade of the livery stable that doubled as a dressing room for the cast. The Injuns attacked the Fort Fun stagecoach every thirty minutes. They were a bored group, sitting and talking about what they would be doing, where they would be, at the same time the next day. There were more than a dozen stagecoach attacks remaining in their run at Fort Fun, and they would tie on the loincloths and apply the warpaint to whoop it up for the customers, but their hearts were not in it.

"How, Black Bart," an Injun said at the train robber's arrival.

"How yourself," Black Bart said.

"Where you headed when this day is done?" the Injun asked.

"South," Black Bart said. "To the Ocutla, Florida, Wild West Review."

"What role?" asked another Injun, with an incongruous and freckled Irish face. He dyed his red hair black and was called O'Geronimo by everybody.

"I am Sneaky Pete," Black Bart said.

"How's the pay?"

"Ugh," Black Bart said and the Injuns laughed. The pay would be $198 a week, a mean step down from Fort Fun. But the Ocutla Wild West Review could hire two dozen Sneaky Petes at half that and regarded itself as a benefactor of the indigent arts for paying so much.

Black Bart walked the bicycle to the rear of the stable and locked it with a chain to a downspout. Dale was intimidated by the Injuns, with their braided hair and headbands, naked but for loincloths and moccasins, some of them smoking cigarettes, and stayed behind his father. In a few minutes the Injuns would go into the stable and put on their warpaint for the first show, still an hour off.

"One more day to go, Bart," said O'Geronimo.

Black Bart smiled. "It's going to be a doozy, too," he said. "Labor Day. All those kids mad about school tomorrow. They'll try and lynch me, you watch. Today, today I wish I was an Injun."

"You're a star," O'Geronimo said. "Why would you want to join up with us half-naked savages?"

"Safety in numbers. I'm just a low-down, despicable train-robber and those kids are going to want my hide." The Injuns laughed. Black Bart asked, "Any of you going to Ocutla?"

"I don't think so, Bart," O'Geronimo said. "I heard Feeney, the blacksmith, I heard he had a job down there."

"Joel Finch, too," Black Bart said. "I'd travel with him, but he is not a sane man behind the wheel."

"You haven't heard?" O'Geronimo asked.

"What haven't I heard?"

"Finch struck out for New York City last night or this morning," O'Geronimo said.

"Yeah?"

"He didn't say anything to you?"

"Finch talked all the time about New York," Black Bart said. He regretted having his son along. The boy was expecting a good time. But for the moment Black Bart saw Dale only as a deterrent to his expressing his anger, disappointment, and jealousy. "The guy finally took the step," Black Bart mused.

"He had work, Bart," O'Geronimo said gently.

"Yeah?"

"A commercial. One of those electronic-calculator companies."

"Greer Electronics," said another Injun. "They ain't been selling too well. That calculator jazz is just a fad. Person's got to know in his head how to add and divide."

"He had a play audition lined up, too," O'Geronimo said.

"Broadway?"

"Off," O'Geronimo said, and this made Black Bart feel spiteful, but better.

He picked up his satchel and ushered Dale to the dressing-room door. At the door he put his hand on the boy's shoulder.

"Injuns," Black Bart said, "I almost forgot. This is my son, Dale. Dale, the Injuns."

The Injuns all grinned and said "How!" holding their hands up, palms out, until Dale smiled and did the same.

Joel Finch spoke of New York City as if it were constructed entirely of jewels, where diamonds ran in the gutter after it rained, and a man had only to get down and pan for his share. When he was ready, he informed Black Bart and anyone else who cared to listen, he was going to New York to become famous. "I plan to be the toast of the whole goddamn town," he would state, one long arm draped over his wife, Angel's, shoulder, his big feet up on the coffee table of Black Bart's rented house. He was six-foot-five and at Fort Fun he was the engineer of the train Black Bart robbed every thirty minutes. He wore striped bib overalls and an engineer's cap with the bill curled just so. In his overalls pocket was a red kerchief.

He was twenty-eight, two years younger than Black Bart. They were oddly matched friends. Their acting ambitions, Joel's fierce and outspoken, Black Bart's subdued but no less intense, and the competition they engendered pulled the two together rather than apart. Joel made a frequent point of telling Black Bart how slim his chances for success were because he had a child, whom Joel referred to as "The Anchor."

"That is it in a nutshell, Bart," Joel said. "You've got 'The Anchor' sleeping in that bedroom and he's got you so you're going nowhere."

"Be quiet, Joel," Angel said.

"He knows I'm right," Joel said to his wife. "Don't you, B.B.? The moment 'The Anchor' was born Bart signed on for a life of playing Black Bart in Wild West shows all over the country. Having a kid cuts off all the options. There's no chance of you taking a risk anymore."

"Having a child is a risk," Julie said.

"You think so? It shouldn't be. If and when we have kids we won't regard it as a risk." Joel reminded Black Bart, with his long, thin arms spread over the back of the couch, of a confident bird expounding upon flight. His hair was thinning and drawing back off his forehead. His face was narrow and angular with brown eyes huge and (Black Bart hated to admit) expressive. He was handsome in a smug way.

"Raising a child is a risk," Julie insisted.

"Nah," Joel said. "No more than raising a cat. Or living any life as well as possible."

"If you care about something, love something, then you are taking a risk," Julie said.

"Granted," Joel said. "But what's it get you if you can't do what you want? I was talking career risks, anyway."

Julie looked to Black Bart for corroboration, for some manner of support.

"We're satisfied with the life we lead," Black Bart said.

"You sound so sure of that," Joel said.

"I am, we are," Black Bart said.

"You talk about wanting to be an actor. This crap we do every day at Fort Fun isn't acting. I quake at the sight of Black Bart come to rob my train again. I've got quaking down pat. You talk acting and as long as I've known you you've talked acting. But now you're thirty and your little boy is almost seven and what do you have? Dale is a great—"

"Damnit, you're driving"—Black Bart shouted the first words, but then Julie laid a cautioning hand on his and he brought his voice to the opposite register, whispering harshly —"you're driving a goddamn train! I don't see your name on any marquees!"

"The option is there, B.B. I haven't spent my entire summer goosing that silly engine. I've been working my career angles very hard."

"Auditioning over the phone?" Black Bart asked.

"We'll see," Joel said. "To me, having a kid is the same as giving up. You're passing the ring to the kid. You're saying, 'I've done all I can do, it's your turn to try, kid.' "

"At the end of the season you'll pack up and drive to Ocutla with the rest of us," Black Bart said.

"We'll see," Joel said.

Cube Jordan came into the dressing room while Black Bart was pulling on his cold, clammy black trousers. Dale stood by like a knight's valet, prepared to hand Black Bart the next piece of his costume.

Jordan slammed through the door without knocking, just the way he entered every other door in Fort Fun. He owned the place, had built it from nothing to its present glory, went his reasoning, and therefore no door within those high walls was not open to him. The story was still told of the time Jordan unhesitatingly chased his fourth wife into a women's lavatory, clearing that small, airless cubicle like a hornet. That had been a few years back. Cube Jordan was on his sixth wife.

He wore each day a very elegant white suit with matching vest and silver-tipped scarlet string tie. He patrolled his domain with an unquestioned, courtly stride, his keen black eyes missing nothing (and if he happened to discover an employee of his dawdling he would casually remove the string tie and sing it across the boy's or girl's unsuspecting buttocks, the snap of the silver tips and the shout of the chastised reaching the ear simultaneously). And though his boots (also white) kicked up the hot dust of summer afternoons, that white suit was forever pristine and sharp. On hotter days he shaded his head with a wide-brimmed white hat, inserted in its red band the tail feather of a hawk. He was a rich man with a single wish: that summer be eternal. Even in winter he spent most of his melancholy day at Fort Fun, cleaning, polishing, repairing, caressing his domain and dreaming of the thaw and the new season.

"Black Bart, you old outlaw!" Jordan roared. "Are you going to send them out in a blaze of glory?" He was as tall and lean as Joel, and just as handsome, but in a different way; handsome the way Mark Twain was handsome.

"I hope to, sir," Black Bart said. He gestured to Dale. "This is my son, Dale. Dale, Mr. Jordan."

"Call me Cube," Jordan said, and he and the boy shook hands.

Jordan sat on the dressing-room bench.

"This is the saddest day of the year for me," he admitted abruptly. "Tomorrow this time, everybody'll be gone but me. Like kids going off for good."

"There'll be another season," Black Bart said.

"That's for darn sure, son!" Jordan burst out happily. "I've been in this business twenty-eight years and that's what I've always found can keep me going from one year to the next. Tomorrow, when this Fort Fun of mine is just as empty as can be, I'll be sad near to crying. But I can say to myself—there'll be an opening day coming around soon. Anything you do, no matter how much you love doing it, will get tiresome. I'm talking hobbies, sex, wives here, son. That is true. But I'll never get tired of Fort Fun. I'm surprised people don't come back day after day. I can't imagine why we ever have a slow day."

"It won't be slow today," Black Bart said.

"That's for darn sure, son! This place is going to be alive with folks today, you can bet on that!" He cackled and said, "And all of them are going to want a piece of Black Bart! They're going to want to take a piece of the bad guy home with them to keep 'em warm in the winter."

"I'm afraid you're right," Black Bart said.

" 'Course I'm right. Why do you think Black Barts never come back?"

"They don't?"

"Ain't had one come back yet. I don't think you'll be any different. They only remember the last day of the season and that convinces 'em being Black Bart was not so great after all."

"I've enjoyed it," Black Bart said.

Jordan tapped Black Bart lightly on the side of the head and said, "You keep that thought, then. Maybe you'll be the first. And one more thing. That no-good Joel Finch skipped on me this morning. You know anything about that?"

"Only what I've heard," Black Bart said.

"I wish him only poor luck and ill health," Jordan said vehemently. "No man deserves success who can't stop in and shake hands goodbye with his old boss. Now I got to find a new engineer." Then he was out the way he had come in, with a rush of wind and a slamming door.

At the halfway point of the Fort Fun railroad, where the track swung around and headed back toward the start, was a carefully arranged pile of boulders. Hidden behind these boulders Black Bart sat astride his horse, Eggplant. The horse was purple-black with a handsome patch of white on his forehead and a deceiving fire in his eye. Eggplant was the best actor in Fort Fun. He had played the same role day after day for eleven seasons and he snorted and flared his eyes and ripped at the ground with his hoofs just as furiously as he had his first day.

The black silk kerchief covered all but Black Bart's eyes. The train approached with its tinny engine amplified through a loudspeaker to give the impression of great power under tenuous rein. Black Bart pressed his hat tighter on his head. He thought about Jordan's observation that no Black Bart ever returned: Were they buried on the spot? Were they carted off to some windblown Boot Hill for phony villains?

Black Bart drew his six-shooters. Eggplant brought his head up when Black Bart's knees pinched his waist. The reins were tied around the saddle horn. Then Black Bart heard his cue, a long, arrogant blast on the train whistle, and he and Eggplant rode out from behind the boulders, Black Bart firing blanks into the sky.

The engine steamed into the bend and Black Bart saw the kids onboard wide-eyed with excitement and delight at his appearance. He saw the sheriff, an agile ex-stuntman named Frank, in his seat at the rear of the train. He saw his son looking confused and scared.

But rather than coming to a halt, as it had every thirty minutes for the entire summer season, the train chugged by without slowing, as if thumbing its nose at the villain on horseback. And though some of the kids hollered at the engineer (a kid of nineteen or twenty Black Bart had not seen before) the train rounded some trees and another pile of boulders and was gone.

Black Bart put away his six-shooters. He pulled down the kerchief and wiped his hand over his face. Soon the notes of the player piano in the saloon reached him. He and Eggplant sat a little longer. Black Bart was not thinking of the new engineer or of the mistake he had made by not stopping. Riding up on the train, Black Bart had been reminded of Joel Finch, and with the train gone the image remained. Joel would soon be in New York, soon be sitting in front of a makeup mirror before doing his pocket-calculator commercial. It was truly "small potatoes," as Joel had said of every acting job he had ever had, but it was also "small potatoes with a future," and Black Bart did not have to think hard to know he was jealous. But the image of Joel leaving for New York made Black Bart feel righteous and clean; he had shown up for the last day of work, he had seen the season through to its close. Also, he felt left behind.

A phone rang behind the boulders.

There was a small hut back there with a sink, a phone, a small icebox filled with jugs of water and an occasional beer, a cot, a radio, some food for the horse, a first-aid kit. Black Bart answered the phone.

"The new engineer didn't stop," Black Bart said at once.

"Black Bart?" It was Cicero. He ran the railroad from the other end.

"Yeah, this is Bart. The train didn't stop."

"You're telling me," Cicero moaned. "We got a new engineer. Just a punk. I guess you heard Finch took off."

"Yeah, I heard," Black Bart said.

"That's tough."

"Why's that tough?"

"Well, you know," Cicero said. "You and Finch was buddies, I thought. There seemed to be something between you and him. A little rivalry. I don't know. It's just tough."

"You see a little boy there who looks lost?"

"Sure, your kid. Jordan pointed him out. Bart, I didn't mean—"

"Put him on," Black Bart said.

"I got to put 'em all on again. They're making a stink they didn't get to beat up on Black Bart."

"No. Put him on the phone."

"Yeah. OK. Wait."

In a moment Dale came on the line. "It's your pop," Black Bart heard Cicero say.

"Dale?"

"What?" the boy said softly.

"It's me," Black Bart said. "The man who drives the train forgot to stop. So you get back on and the next time around he'll stop. OK?"

Dale was silent.

"Do you want to go again?"

Still Dale said nothing.

"Did you see me?" Black Bart asked.

"Yeah."

"Did you like it?"

"I was scared."

"It is supposed to scare people, Dale. You know I'm not like that, don't you?"

"Oh," Dale said. Black Bart thought he said no.

"I'm not," he said. But there was no immediate way to prove this so he said, "You get back on the train next time."

"OK," Dale said, and a moment later Cicero was on the line.

"See he gets on the train," Black Bart said.

"Sure, Bart," Cicero said. He lowered his voice. "You're going to have company this trip. The Cube."

The train blew its cocky whistle and Black Bart and Eggplant galloped out from behind the boulders with six-shooters blazing. The train brakes screamed. The children and adults shrieked with excitement. The train came to a halt, hissing and steaming as if personally affronted.

Black Bart pointed his revolvers menacingly at the passengers. They all had their hands up and were smiling. He could not see his son and worried that Cicero had forgotten to put him back on the train. Eggplant snickered and pranced.

"Throw down the mailbag!" Black Bart ordered. The engineer, the same kid, his hands halfheartedly in the air, reached behind his seat for the canvas mailbag and tossed it out onto the ground. Black Bart looked at it and then at the passengers. He saw the sheriff sitting in the rear of the train. His hat was pulled low over his eyes and he was yawning. Black Bart still did not see his son. Cube Jordan was sitting beside the sheriff.

None of the passengers, save the very young, was frightened. They were waiting for their cue. One brawny kid, maybe fourteen years old, looked vaguely familiar to Black Bart, as if he had seen the kid early in the season and over the course of the summer the kid had reached manhood. He was tall and stocky with a pugnacious, exultant face. He was poised on the balls of his feet awaiting the command to get Black Bart.

Black Bart dismounted. The passengers leaned toward him; the line of cars even seemed to tip in his direction. Black Bart holstered one six-shooter. He wound a leather strap around the hammer, tied it securely so that in the coming melee the revolver would not fall loose. He crouched over the mailbag, his other six-shooter trained on the passengers, the barrel square on the big kid's forehead. Black Bart hesitated just a moment to look one more time for Dale. His son was not on the train. He stood up with the mailbag.

"Get this train out of here," Black Bart commanded.

There was a rustle of protest from the passengers, an angry murmur of disgust that perhaps the format had been changed and Black Bart would be allowed to escape unchallenged. The engineer dutifully activated the loudspeaker and filled the air with the grumping of the priming engine. Black Bart swung up into the saddle. He fired a shot into the air.

This was the sheriff's cue. He jumped from the rear of the train with his gun drawn and shouted, "We can't let Black Bart steal the Fort Fun mail!" Black Bart leveled a shot at him but, of course, he missed. The sheriff returned the fire. On the first shot Black Bart threw his six-shooter over the boulders as if it had been shot out of his hand. On the second shot Black Bart dropped the mailbag and slapped his hand to his shoulder, spun out of the saddle, hit the ground feet first, and dropped at once to his knees.

Eggplant was then between Black Bart and the train, but as the horse moved out of the way he revealed a sight so unnerving that Black Bart almost wanted to draw his gun. The train was emptying in a holiday wave of children angry at the end of summer and they were led by the big kid, who covered the ground between himself and Black Bart in long, loping strides, his arm drawing back, his hand knotting into a fist, his teeth flashing in a cheerless smile. He uncorked a wicked right at Black Bart's head but Black Bart saw it coming and ducked and the whistling fist flew past. The momentum of the missed blow left the kid off balance and Black Bart simply put both hands on the kid's waist and tossed him over his head. Black Bart would have liked to turn to see the kid land flat on his back but there was no time. The mob descended.

The sheriff let the kids beat on Black Bart for a full minute before firing a shot in the air and announcing in a voice that brooked no rebellion, "Everybody back on the train! Black Bart's had enough!"

The pack dispersed, sweating and grumbling. The engineer barked the horn three times. Black Bart was handcuffed and his gunbelt removed. The sheriff tossed the mailbag onto the train.

"Thanks for your help, folks!" the sheriff said. "I'll take Black Bart to jail myself. You enjoy the rest of your stay in Fort Fun!"

The big kid struggled to his knees, then to his feet. His face was nearly without color. "I'll be back, Black Bart!" the kid wheezed. "I'll get you before this day is done!" Then he spat on Black Bart's boot. When the kid was onboard, the train began to move. Its whistle hooted triumphantly. The sheriff waved farewell to the passengers. A few of them cheered.

"They truly love you, Bart," he said out of the corner of his mouth.

Before the train had gone very far Cube Jordan dropped off the rear end and walked back to them.

"It's a hell of a life, ain't it, Bart?" he said.

When the train was out of sight the sheriff removed the handcuffs and returned the gunbelt. Black Bart brushed himself off.

"You OK?" Jordan asked.

"They tried to kill me!"

"Nah," Jordan said. "They're good kids. They just know this is their last chance to let the sputum run before school starts. Beating on Black Bart is a true Labor Day tradition in these parts."

"Where was Dale? I told Cicero to put him on again." An ache had begun in Black Bart's back. A welt spread across the bridge of his nose, and his ribs felt as if they had been hit each in turn like xylophone bars. The sheriff had gone into the hut for a drink of water and when he came out he waved and began the short walk back to the beginning of the line.

"I took certain liberties in that regard, Bart," Jordan said. "I told Cicero to let the boy help take tickets. And I must say he showed a real talent for it. Learned quicker than Cicero did. He liked the idea of helping. You give him enough to do at home?"

"He wanted to see me work," Black Bart insisted.

"You wanted him to see you work," Jordan said. "He seen you once when the train went past and I think that was enough for him. You scared the boy, Bart!"

"He's seen the suit a thousand times," Black Bart protested.

"Sure he has. In the safety of his own home, where he can see you turn from his pa into Black Bart a little at a time. A man in black on horseback firing six-guns is another matter. Besides, I did it for you, too. It's not good for a boy to see his pa get beat up on a regular basis!" Jordan chuckled. He sat down on the bench outside the hut. Black Bart went inside and shut the door and switched on the light over the sink. He took his six-shooters out and replaced the blanks he had fired. Then he poured a cup of water from a jug in the icebox and sat down for a moment. Through the door he heard Jordan humming. And in a few minutes he heard the whoop of the train whistle announcing its departure. It would arrive in six minutes. Jordan tapped on the door.

"You're on," he said.

Black Bart inspected his costume. It was gritty and realistic. There was a rip in his shirt. There was the light of a desperado in his eyes. He walked out of the hut and climbed up into the saddle.

"I'd be proud to have you back next season, Bart," Jordan said. They shook hands. Then Jordan returned to the bench by the hut to await the train's arrival.

On cue, Black Bart and Eggplant rode out into the open. Black Bart fired his warning shots. The train was filled again, and sitting in the front seat was the big kid. Black Bart wondered how long his money would hold out, or if he had a patron.

"Throw down your mailbag!" Black Bart ordered.

The engineer threw the mailbag onto the ground at Eggplant's feet.

Black Bart dismounted. The moment his boots touched the ground the big kid was off the train and running at him. Black Bart fired a shot in the air. On came the kid. He was snarling. His punch sailed past Black Bart's ear and into Eggplant's thick and immobile flank. Something cracked. The kid screamed. Black Bart could hear Cube Jordan hooting behind the boulders.

There were just four children on the last train of the season and one of them was Black Bart's son. The four children, three boys and a girl, were evidently the shyest of all the children who had passed through Fort Fun that day, those most disposed to staying out of crowds and out of the way of louder and more aggressive children.

When the engineer threw the mailbag out for the last time the four children collected in a knot by the sheriff at the back of the train. Black Bart jumped down from the saddle.

"Are you just going to stand there and let me steal Fort Fun's mail?" he asked the four children.

Yes, apparently they were. Like good, frightened citizens at the scene of a crime where they have no stake and no loyalty, they stared at the villain in black and at his black horse and made no move to protect that which did not belong to them. They were small, sensible people who only wanted Black Bart to mount up and leave them to complete their short, harrowing journey.

But Black Bart would not let them go.

He put away his six-shooters and went to the side of the train. He pulled down his black kerchief and smiled at his son and then at all of them. Black Bart considered riding the train in but he had to look after Eggplant and so he shook hands with each of the children and then lifted his son to the ground. It was late afternoon of a late-summer day and his son's small face was sunburned and dusty from a day in the ticket booth. Fort Fun would be closing in a half-hour. Black Bart handed the mailbag to the little girl and said to the sheriff, "I'm going straight." He motioned to the engineer and the kid threw the train into gear and it ground away from the two of them, father and son, without fanfare or whistle.

Black Bart bought three hot dogs from the vendor, the last three hot dogs of the season, the vendor a tiny man with a Wild West look in his eyes who clapped Black Bart on the elbow and said, "Bless you, Bart, it's a good omen to end the season selling in threes."

The hot dogs were cold and delicious. Black Bart and Dale sat on the dressing-room steps eating and saying goodbye to Injuns and buglers and blacksmiths and stagecoach drivers. Some asked Black Bart about Joel Finch and he told them they knew as much as he did.

Then Black Bart and Dale walked to a water pump on the other side of the stable and discovered their bicycle had been stolen. The chain that bound it to the downspout had been cut.

"Who'd want an old bike like that?" Black Bart wondered.

"Maybe a kid in a hurry," Dale said.

"I'll change, then we can start walking," Black Bart said.

Cube Jordan was in the dressing room, standing by a large canvas laundry-hamper on wheels. The Fort Fun actors undressed and deposited their costumes in the hamper. Next to the hamper was a box as tall as Dale for accessories.

As Black Bart entered the dressing room Jordan handed him a check.

"Here's your last week's pay, Bart," Jordan said. He sounded utterly unhappy having to say those words. But Black Bart barely noticed.

"I asked for cash," he said.

"That there's good," Jordan said.

"I know it is, sir, but we, my son and my wife and me, we're heading for Florida tonight and there won't be any place open to cash a check this size at night."

"I'm sorry about that," Jordan said. "But I've got to have a record of my payroll."

"I talked to Brenda. She said it would be OK."

"You did? I'm sorry about that, too. Brenda's my wife's niece. She probably forgot what you said the minute you left the office."

"I need cash, Cube," Black Bart repeated.

Jordan fingered the ends of a bountiful mustache that tumbled over the corners of his mouth. The color of river foam, it would go pure white if he lived long enough; he was sixty-nine. He was not an intractable man but he liked to keep a firm, organizational hand on his life and he expected others to do the same.

"Git damn, Bart," Jordan said. "This is some fix. But I'm not convinced it is my fix. I paid you by check all summer, and have you had trouble converting those checks to cash? No, I don't think you did. Now you want cash on the last day? I think you're just guilty of poor planning, Bart."

"I thought it was settled," Black Bart said.

Jordan waved that idea away. "Brenda is a little slow picking up mental ground balls and she's my wife's niece. She was foisted on me like half the other cretins I'm related to by blood or bondage who I've provided honorable employment for. I'm sorry you had to find that out under such inconvenient circumstances but that is just the way this life travels."

"My boy starts school day after tomorrow," Black Bart said.

Jordan shook his head in admiration. "You don't quit, do you? He's a bright boy. He can miss a day."

Black Bart thought of Julie waiting packed and ready, the rented house clean and empty and cavernlike in its treatment of footsteps and echoes. He thought, too, of the stolen bicycle. The theft of it now served Black Bart's purpose. He and Dale would have to walk over the hills to the place marked by the red rock where they had hidden the other bicycle. From there they would pedal home with Black Bart's knees crushed under the handlebars of the smaller bike. It would take a long time. And it would be dark soon. How could they be expected to start a long journey after such a day?

Black Bart skimmed his black hat into the box. The black kerchief followed. Then the black vest. He unhooked the spurs and gave them to Dale and the boy put them in the box.

"Where do you want the boots?" Black Bart asked.

"Leave 'em by your locker, Bart," Jordan said. "Put the six-guns by the boots."

Then Black Bart removed the shirt and trousers and they were damp with his sweat. Maybe they would finally dry over the winter. When he held the trousers up to a window, light came through the seat. He was standing in his underwear in the September dusk, and when he threw the shirt and trousers into the hamper, he was Black Bart no more.

No, now he was Sneaky Pete. He would wear a false mustache until he grew one of his own and a foolish, drooping wide-brimmed hat. Every thirty minutes he would stage a fistfight with a lawman who sported a clean jaw and a flat belly, and though Sneaky Pete would lose every one of the fights, hundreds over the course of the season, the audience would frequently take his side and cheer him on.

1-800-Your Boy

Marilyn and Lake were downstairs playing Mouse-trap in the sun when the first call came. A woman, nervous, said to me, "I saw your boy in a dream. I just woke up. Give me a minute." She swallowed something, a bubbling at the other end of the line, and smacked her lips. "I remember railroad tracks. And a tree with leaves, leaves just turning color. Red and . . . red and gold."

"Pardon?" I said.

"Your boy. He was dressed in blue jeans. Blue jeans with a patch on his . . . *left* knee. A black, black T-shirt. He was in a dream. I *saw* him. Railroad tracks. A tree. I've probably been no help, no help—" she chuckled derisively "—at all."

I ran down the three flights of stairs to the courtyard. Marilyn and Lake sat facing each other over a picnic table. Two redheads intent on the complex process of putting the game board together, they had come downstairs at just the right time to sit in the sun. With his coppery hair and light blue eyes, Lake looked like he belonged to Marilyn, but his mother, who also resembled Marilyn, lived an hour away.

Our new apartment was on the top floor of a four-story red-brick cube, from whose center had been hollowed a charmless little courtyard. Management provided two picnic tables, and a lawn that could be mowed in three passes. Now, late in the summer, sunlight found its way to the bottom of the box canyon for only minutes a day, and Marilyn and Lake had made a game of calculating the light's arrival and the duration of its stay. Marilyn was confident enough to wear her swimsuit, a little two-piece that drew phantom wolf whistles from deep in the shadowy apartments.

"What is it?" Marilyn asked. She indicated with a dip of her shoulder that there was room for me on her bench, but it was Lake I wanted to sit beside. He was busy with a small green plastic man who stood poised to dive at one end of a teeter-totter. By tapping the opposite end, Lake propelled the man through the air and into a vat.

"Nothing's wrong. I wondered what you were doing. Can't I take some sun with you?" I asked. Lake's shoulders were smooth and solid beneath my hand. Lost in the game, he paid no attention to me.

"We're glad to have you," Marilyn said.

I could see the street through the tunnel from the court-yard. Doors opened off the tunnel: a door to the manager's apartment, another to the laundry room, and a third door I'd never looked behind.

"I wish I could see you from the apartment," I said, looking up, catching the sunlight in my eye.

"We're fine," Marilyn said. She rubbed her hand along my arm. The back of her hand was coated with freckles, as was most of the rest of her. Her freckles amazed me, some of the places I found them. Knowing that Lake was safe, that Marilyn was with him, made me antsy with love for them both; for Marilyn in a particular way, for Lake in the blind way that allowed him to pay me no heed, even as I scratched his back.

"Have you heard from Daisy?" I asked.

Lake's head came up. "Mom?"

"Yeah."

"Why would I hear from her?" Marilyn asked.

"I thought maybe she called. You forgot to tell me."

Marilyn took back her hand. "I give you all your messages," she said.

"I just haven't heard from her. Usually I hear from her."

"Mom?"

"*Yes,*" I said, dismayed by the longing in his voice.

That courtyard held sounds, moved them around, made them more than they were, so when I heard a phone ring, I had no idea where it was coming from.

"That's ours," Marilyn said.

"How do you know?" I asked, but believing her, rising.

"I recognize the sound and location," she said, pointing to our window.

I was out of breath when I got to the door, and needed a while to get my key out, but the phone ringing in the apartment projected a patience, a willingness to ring for as long as necessary.

A man this time said, "I want reward information before I say anything. And I'm not telling you anything for less than five hundred dollars. Is that clear? Now . . . what are you paying?"

"For what?" I asked.

"For your kid, you cheap dick," he said. "Isn't your kid worth five hundred dollars to you?"

"My—my son is sitting right in front of me," I said, though I was nervous again out of sight of Lake. "I see him with my own two eyes."

"You're lying. *I* know where he is," the man said. "You

want him back, but you're too cheap to offer a reward. Guys like you make me sick."

By pressing my eye as close to the kitchen window as possible, I could see Marilyn's hair smouldering in the last of the sunlight. But I couldn't see Lake. Marilyn was speaking matter-of-factly to someone. She gave no hint of being party to a kidnapping.

Daisy did not want custody of Lake, and then she did. By then the divorce was final, and Lake was mine. She wanted to press the fight all over again in court, but she couldn't afford a lawyer. She asked me to retain one for her, but I refused. With what I'm paid to teach junior high school science, I didn't have money for a lawyer either. I feared that she might persuade one of her boyfriends to put up the money, and then I would be forced to hire a lawyer of my own.

She saw Lake every other week, and he spent one weekend a month with her. I dreaded those overnight visits. I didn't trust Daisy. She went for the quick fix in their relationship, trying to win Lake's love with nearly unlimited sugar and an absence of discipline. He returned to me moody and confused, a terror for two or three days afterward, such a pain in the ass that his teachers told me they could tell when he had spent the weekend with his mother.

Our routine was for Daisy to drop Lake at school after his visit, and I would pick him up in the afternoon. Inevitably, because he was in a bad mood, because he knew he could score with it, he asked, "Where's Mom?"

One Monday morning I was called out of class by a messenger who spoke of an emergency phone call, and I sprinted down the halls to the office. Lake's school had phoned to report that Daisy had called. Lake was sick and wouldn't be at school that day.

I dialed Daisy's number and nobody answered. She was already in violation of her visitation terms: if Lake had to miss school after her weekend, she was required to bring him home at the time she would have dropped him off at school.

They got a sub for me, and I went home and phoned Daisy again. No answer.

"It'll be all right," Marilyn said. "She just forgot the rules. She probably wanted to play hooky with him."

"She knows the rules."

I was certain she had taken Lake away. She had gone on the run with him, emptying her bank account, packing the car, and vanishing into the landscape. She might have left the instant she took possession of him Friday, and called his school long distance to avoid suspicion for a little longer, to buy another day's flight.

Marilyn urged me to wait, but I called the police. I was switched through a series of people until a patient man listened to my story, but he refused to do anything, even to take my name. What I was experiencing was so common, and my particular case so embryonic in development, that, he implied, I was being a bit of a sissy for calling so soon.

"She's had him two days, nearly three days," I said. "She could get *anywhere* in that time."

"Our projections say you'll have your boy back before sunset," he said. "If you haven't heard from her this time tomorrow, call us back."

I called Daisy's apartment every ten minutes. Marilyn fixed us lunch, coaxed me to eat, and promised, in that sincere and confident manner of hers, that I would get Lake back.

Daisy phoned early in the afternoon. She was crying. She had dropped Lake off at school.

"I was going to take him," she said.

"I know. I've already called the police."

"Oh, great!"

"Don't worry," I said. "They didn't take any information. You aren't wanted."

I considered denying Daisy her weekend visitation rights, but decided against that. The fact that I had broken our agreement might someday be used against me in court. She never explained why she had not run away with Lake. Marilyn said that Daisy realized Lake loved me, that running away with Lake would wrench him for a second time out of the familiar comforts of his life. I believed that Daisy suddenly realized what an inconvenience kidnapping a little boy was and decided she couldn't be bothered.

Marilyn seemed to love Lake. She was always eager to do things with him, to make golfball ice cubes, take him to the park, cook spaghetti, read him a book. I was a little annoyed that he accepted her attention as his due. He seemed to be fully aware that he was lovable, irresistible, to the adults in his life. I wanted Marilyn to love him. I wanted that more than I wanted him to love her. Or her me.

I told her about the two calls. We were in the kitchen drinking beer. Lake was asleep. Out the window the courtyard air hummed after a night of radios, arguments, someone loudly making love somewhere, and conversations strung like clothesline looping from wall to wall.

"Wrong numbers," Marilyn said confidently, anxious to clear the worry from my look. "Someone with a number similar to ours has a missing boy. Those two hit the wrong button."

That was simple to understand and accept. Lake was sleeping soundly in his bed; his young boy's throaty snore was like a machine running on the other side of the wall. My boy was not missing. That was someone else's nightmare.

"That's exactly what happened," Marilyn said.

But I lay on my back after she was asleep and waited for

the phone to ring, convinced the calls were coming to me out of the future, a nightmare of my own I had to look forward to. And a call did come, so early in the morning that I couldn't read the clock even by window light.

"I had . . . another dream," the woman said. "I'm frightened. I don't want to keep dreaming. This time, your boy is in a supermarket. He is standing in an aisle," she said. She paused, and I imagined her trying to see the dream as clearly as she could. "He is in a supermarket aisle. Cookies and crackers on one side. Soups on the other side. He is hungry and he's crying. Somebody is with him. If you could find a store with the aisles laid out like that—that might be a help to the police."

Nearly in a whisper, I said, "Thank you—but I found my boy."

"You did?"

"He came home today."

"But my dreams—" she said. Then, in a clipped voice, she scolded me. "If you found him, take down your signs. Stop getting the rest of us all worked up."

Marilyn scolded me too. "You've done a terrible thing! That woman isn't dreaming about Lake. She's dreaming about the missing boy. What if her dreams are real? Now she'll pay no attention to them. She won't try to make sense of them because she thinks the boy is safe."

"But they were so vague," I said. "A railroad track. A tree. A grocery store."

Marilyn shook her head. "No. No, I took a class in dreams once. That woman was beginning to focus in. Each dream would get more specific. I think you should put an ad in the paper and try to reach her."

She went outside with Lake when the sun was right. She was capable of holding a grudge, and her disapproval of me seemed to infect my son, who gave me a blank glare of disappointment the equal of Marilyn's as they went out the door. I stayed at the kitchen table working on my check-book, the bills, lesson plans for the coming semester. In a couple of weeks I would begin teaching in my fourth school district in four years. Funding dried up wherever I took a job, forcing the lopping off of the new guys. My lessons had an amorphous quality; they never seemed real until kids were in front of me.

I should have been downstairs playing with Lake and Marilyn, but I was waiting for the phone to ring. I wanted the dream woman to call back, convinced that her dreams were so vivid that my boy had to be still missing. I imagined her taking a nap in a dark, warm room, angry with herself for being sleepy in the middle of the day, but stretching out under a crisp sheet, her hair moistening the instant she was asleep. A dream would then come to her, with signs, ad-dresses, directions, and she would have no choice but to call. She wouldn't sleep again until she had.

We took Lake to a carnival that evening, and he walked like a guard between us. The air had the panic of summer's end. Looks of despair stretched the faces of every kid. We went on rides that were easy on our stomachs. I shot baskets. Lake threw darts at balloons. I was determined to win a lion for Marilyn, but the hoop I shot at was barely bigger around than the ball I shot. Lake punctured two balloons in three throws and selected a necklace of pink and green pop-beads, which Marilyn accepted with a kiss of gratitude. Almost at once she warmed up to me, too, taking my arm, pressing it against the side of her breast. She saw something in Lake's sweetness that put me in a better light. I think she knew he loved her, and that made it safe for her to love me again. We stood together while he went for a ride on whirling teacups. I lost sight of him, found him, lost him again. I didn't mention my uneasiness to Marilyn, fearful that it would remind her of the dream woman. But I was relieved when Lake came wobbling off the ride, his face green at the edges, his need for me at the moment absolute. While I steadied him, held his head, found him a cup of ice water, I was reasonably confident I would never lose him.

A woman, not the dream woman, called on Monday. "I saw your boy at the planetarium," she told me. "He was with a man and woman in their forties. He was buying a constellation globe."

I asked her what number she was calling, and the number she was calling was our number.

"But no boy is missing here," I said.

"Why put up the signs?"

"We didn't."

"Somebody did."

"Not us."

"They're all over the tollway," she said. "Your boy's face is everywhere."

"Not my boy's," I said, stressing the point.

Marilyn had me go through the call again for her.

"They're calling our number," I said. "She was very adamant about that."

"Could people go to the trouble of printing up posters, but in their grief not notice that the phone number was wrong?" Marilyn wondered.

"Could the printer take the money of grieving parents—and make a mistake like that?" I asked.

We went for a ride in the evening, the three of us in the front seat, Lake suspicious when his questions about our destination drew no definite answers. We simply got on the tollway, mixed into the traffic headed toward the city, and drove the eleven miles to the first toll plaza.

The posters were there: on the exact-change baskets and on the manned booths. They showed a boy with dark hair and dark eyes, an expression of pre-adolescent ennui at the prospect of being photographed, his grin a tad snide. Not a likable kid, was my first impression.

Above the picture was the thick, black word **missing,** and beneath it the query HAVE YOU SEEN OUR SON? Beneath the picture was his name—DAVID A. RICHARDSON—and the simple plea, nearly a command, CALL 1-800-YOUR BOY.

"They haven't been dialing the 1-800," Marilyn said excitedly.

"What?" Lake said. "Where're we going?"

"YOUR BOY? That's our number?" I tried to picture a telephone, to match letters and numbers.

Marilyn was faster. "Sure. Y is 9. O is 6. U is 8. That's it! That's our number!"

"YOUR BOY," I said.

"Where are we going?" Lake asked.

"Into the city," I said.

"You have to call that number," Marilyn said. "They should know what we know."

"What do we know?"

"About the woman with the dreams. About the couple at the planetarium."

"And I should tell them that I told the dream woman their boy had been found?"

She reached across Lake and rested her hand on my thigh. "It was an honest mistake. But you *must* call."

"How much credence do we give to the reports of people too stupid to dial an 800 number right?" I asked.

"You have to call," she said.

We spent time in the city just walking, to tire out Lake. Both Marilyn and I were anxious to be home. After an hour we headed back. But before I could make the call, a call came to us.

A man told me, "He's dead. I know just where, too. You'll never see him again."

"Give us proof," I said.

"I don't need proof. He's gone for good."

"What about the reward?"

"It's too late for that. Your boy is dead."

I hung up, which was probably a mistake, but I did not want to listen to him any longer. And he had our number. He was free to call us at any time with reports of my son's death.

"He said the boy's dead," I told Marilyn.

"Call the number. They should know."

I dialed the number and got a busy signal, and Marilyn put her hand on mine and said, "Don't forget the 1-800."

"I didn't."

"Try again."

A man answered. His voice was chipper, enthusiastic.

"My name is Burt McKenzie," he said. "I'm handling the phones for the Richardsons. Do you have any information about their son?"

I cleared my throat. I told him, "I don't know. But I thought I should report some calls we've been getting."

"We appreciate that. Do you mind if we tape-record this conversation?"

"No."

"Good. Could you tell me your name, please?"

"My name is Phil. Our phone number is the same as your 800 number without the 1-800. We've been getting some calls from people who forget to dial the 1-800."

Burt McKenzie laughed appreciatively. "People, huh? What did they say?"

"One guy asked for a reward. He wouldn't tell me anything until he heard about the reward," I said.

"We get that, too. Ignore him."

"A woman said she saw your boy at the planetarium," I said. "He was with a man and a woman in their forties."

"The planetarium in the city?"

"I think so. She didn't say."

"We'll check that out," he said. "That might be a good place for some posters, come to think of it. Lots of parents go through there. Let me write that down. Plan-et-ar-ium. That's a big help, Phil."

"Thanks. And we got calls from a woman who said she saw your boy in a dream," I said.

"A dream?"

"Two dreams, actually. One, he was by a railroad track. A tree was nearby, with its leaves changing color. The second one, he was in a grocery store. By the cookies and the soups."

"Not much to go on," Burt McKenzie said.

"I have to be honest, though. I didn't want her calling anymore, so I told her we'd found your boy—my boy—the missing boy. I'm sorry."

"Phil, don't give it another thought," he said. "Sure, we'd be interested in talking to her—but her locations are so general. I don't know what help they could be."

"My girlfriend thinks she was focusing in," I said.

"Maybe," Burt McKenzie said. "I've been running phones now for eight years, Phil, and I've talked to a hundred dreamers, at least. Not one has helped find a kid."

"You do this for a living?" I asked.

"You got children?"

"A boy."

"God forbid he ever disappears, 1-800-FONE GUY. With an F. Enough said about that, Phil. Do you have anything else for us today?"

"One last one. I'm sure it's nothing."

"Shoot."

"Someone called today and said your boy was dead."

Burt McKenzie paused and then said, "Cruel people, Phil. There's a million of them. We get calls from a guy who pretends he's connected to the investigation. He's called four times to ask us to come down and identify the remains of a body that matches the description of David. He's full of details. He gets off on describing the condition of the body."

"Have any calls helped you?" I asked.

"Things have quieted down. We had a rush of calls after the posters went up on the tollways. Nothing of any use, though. People just like to talk, Phil. They like to know it's not their kid."

We were eating dinner when Daisy came to the door. She stepped into the kitchen, blinking, a big purse hanging from her shoulder.

"You cut your hair," Marilyn observed. "I like it. It brings out your eyes."

"You think so?" Daisy said, primping.

"It's great. Would you like some dinner? We have plenty."

"No, thanks. Really."

"Have some, Mom," Lake said.

Daisy allowed herself to be drawn into our family far enough to hook her bag over a chair and sit down. She let Marilyn pour her a cup of coffee, but refused the offer of sugar and milk, though I knew she took both. She was standing her ground on small matters, picking those spots where she felt confident to resist. Her eyes never fell on me.

"Did you pack your swim trunks?" she asked Lake.

He didn't know. In turning his head inquiringly to Marilyn, who had packed his suitcase, he wounded Daisy more deeply than I ever could.

"It's packed," Marilyn said gently, aware herself.

"Because we're going to a hotel this weekend—and you'll have lots of chances to swim," Daisy said.

"Ooh. That sounds like such fun," Marilyn said.

"Which hotel?" I asked.

Daisy fished in her cavernous bag and came out with a piece of paper. "The Holidome," she said. "Here's the phone number and the room number. We're all checked in, Laker. A room on the pool."

"Neat-o," Marilyn said.

"We have a new number—speaking of numbers," I said. I got a pencil from the drawer by the phone and wrote it down for her.

"We were getting some weird calls," Marilyn explained.

"Breathers?" Daisy asked.

"Stuff like that."

"I get about two a month. Just hang up on them."

"These were pretty persistent," Marilyn said. "It's easier to change the number than worry every time the phone rings."

"Were these dirty calls?" Daisy pressed, intrigued.

"I want to do this to you. I want to do that," Marilyn said, looking to me. "You know."

"And Lake answers the phone too," I said.

Marilyn went with Lake into his room to get his suitcase. I heard him brush his teeth and use the toilet. Daisy and I did not speak to each other. Soon enough Marilyn and Lake were back.

"I'll drop him at school Monday," Daisy said.

"School's still a week off. Bring him back here."

"Sure," Daisy said. "Ready, kid? The pool awaits."

Lake passed out kisses in somber fashion; one for Marilyn on the cheek, one for me on the chin. He carried his own bag.

I listened to them descend the stairs, Daisy's voice metallic with forced cheer. For an instant my heart went out to her: the pain of awkwardness she must fight through each time she had her son to herself.

Marilyn asked me a question, but I was concentrating on the sounds of their departure. They were in the courtyard now. Daisy's voice came up breathless and more relaxed, the exertion of the climb down relieving some of her anxiety.

"I said, 'Does Lake know how to swim?' "

I didn't answer. Lake was speaking with more animation than I would have wished. His voice faded as they turned into the tunnel, and then he was gone.

With or Without

For the longest time the woods were untouched and Dolph Hjurak lived contentedly in the house he had bought alongside them. His house was small, only six rooms—a bathroom, a kitchen, a living room, and three bedrooms, all on one floor—and in that limited space over nearly thirty-six years he and Elle had raised three girls and two boys.

All but one of the children had moved away. The girls all had married, one twice, but among them had produced no grandchildren. Kevin, the oldest child, had a son, though no wife anymore, and deposited the child with Dolph and Elle every morning before work.

Carl, the youngest, was still at home. He was in high school and in his spare time worked on dead cars, four in the front and two in back, behind the dogs' pen. He had filled his sisters' old room with spare parts and his tools.

He was in back one morning very early, and in the relative quiet that followed his filling of the dogs' bowls he heard a chainsaw rev. He went around front. His father already was there. He wore his gloves and carried his pipe and pouch. They walked to where the woods began. In the narrow light among the trees they saw two men working in yellow hard-hats. One man studied papers; the other sized a tree.

The blade was put to the tree and resistance made the man retreat momentarily, the hesitation signaled by a deepening of the saw's one-note song. Then the work resumed. The man with the plans folded them casually under his arm and stepped aside when the tree began to fall in his direction.

"Go inside. Breakfast's ready," Dolph said. "Are you finished with the dogs?"

"Yes," Carl said.

"I'll come in in a little bit."

Elle took Carl's jacket at the door. "What? Tell me," she said.

"They are cutting down trees."

"This would happen some day, your father said," Elle told him. "His greatest fear, he said it was."

"To have neighbors?"

"To have . . . people who don't understand him living on his front stoop."

Dolph paused in the shadows to get his pipe going, to swirl his head in smoke. The saw hurt his ears. A pickup truck the color of new sod was parked in the road. Other men had come to the woods more than three years before and cut down a number of trees and sectioned them and taken them away. With Carl and Kevin he made forays in the dark with the wheelbarrow to scavenge for wood, taking away so much that the three of them stacked wood against two walls of their house all the way up to the eaves, where the Christmas lights hung year-round.

With the trees felled, a bulldozer had come and cleared the stumps, and when that was finished a grader smoothed the shaved land and men poured the concrete form for a cul-de-sac. In little more than a week the road was in, blacktopped and perfect. He could hear it hiss on cool nights.

Dolph expected the clearing operations to expand to the

individual lots and then for new houses to rise. The preparation of the road had moved with unmistakable urgency. It was urgency pushed, he knew, by the presence of money; a presence especially keen to Dolph, who had little. He expected the foundations for the first houses to be completed before school began. But after the road was in, the work stopped. He waited each day for the men to return but he never saw them again. His calls to the village to discover the source of the delay were fruitless. No one would reveal a thing (even over the phone, he assumed, they could tell he had no money, and therefore deserved no answers) until one afternoon in the week before Labor Day a woman in the building department said offhandedly that the owner of the parcels had run into trouble with his financing.

"The fellow had money behind him," he told Elle. "And then he didn't."

Now, three years later, the work resumed. Dolph counted four trees down. The man with the papers saw Dolph emerge from the woods and allowed him a polite smile. His hand rose to the nubby bill of his hard hat, but then his eyes returned to the sheets he held. He was safe from questioning in the painful air around the saw.

Dolph did not approach the man directly, but stood a few steps to the side, and behind, where he could smoke his pipe and watch both men work. A plume of white sawdust spurted from each cut in the tree, the gush softening into a rain as it flew clear. The trees fell almost in silence, with regal grudgingness, sending up a thumping roar only at the very end.

As it happened, Dolph did not speak to the men at all that day. Through the thinning forest he saw Kevin's pickup turn into the driveway and Dolph hurried to greet not his son, but Russell, his grandson.

The dogs were making a racket. Kevin and the boy had gone into the house. Russell was almost three years old, and stood just inside the front door, still in his coat, hat, and mittens. He watched his father smoke a cigarette and wolf down an apple danish Elle had warmed. Dolph snatched off the boy's stocking cap so his hair swirled into an electric peak.

"Papa!" screamed the boy. Dolph, on his knees, enclosed Russell in his arms. Dolph was of the belief that Kevin did not exhibit sufficient interest in his son to be a good father, and therefore he would have to be the boy's saving grace. Kevin had married a girl whose sole virtue, in Dolph's estimation, had been to bring forth one perfect child. She had disappeared soon after. The loss seemed to have affected only Kevin, who, when not working, spent his time and money in search of her, or a woman like her.

"What's going on in the woods?" Kevin asked.

"They're finally clearing those lots," Dolph said. "I suspect they'll finally build on them."

"His worst fear, he says," Elle said. She handed Kevin a spare danish in a brown sack. She had a glass of orange juice and a vitamin out for Russell.

"They must have gotten the financing, is all," Dolph said with a shrug. If he closed his eyes he could see trees falling.

"Can Russ stay here tonight?" Kevin asked.

"Where are you going?"

"To a guy's house I know. He's having a bunch of people over. It'll be a late night."

"Did you pack him a bag?" Dolph asked.

"He can sleep in those clothes. He can use one of my old toothbrushes." Kevin took the glass of orange juice meant for his son, swallowed the juice, kissed Russell on the ear, and rushed out. They heard him curse the dogs.

"Are you hungry, Russell?" Elle asked.

"Yes, I am," the boy said. He scrambled into his chair.

"So your daddy's going to a party tonight," Dolph said.

"A-dolph Hjur-ak," Elle sang.

"And Russell gets to spend all day and all night with his Papa!"

"Also Gram," Elle said.

"Where's the boy's food?" Dolph asked. "Russell is hungry! He's wasting away to nothing! Feel these meatless bones"—and Dolph screwed a finger into the boy's soft ribs, and Russell folded with howls of laughter. When his eyes were busy with the boy, Dolph received a cool look from Elle.

After breakfast Dolph and Russell went back outside. The sun was burning the frost off Carl's cars. Russell wanted to play with the bounding dogs, but Dolph was impatient to return to the woods. The chainsaw wasn't running.

"Come, Russell."

The saw was on the bed of the truck, and the man who had been using it now stood some distance away holding a long staff, the top half of which was fluorescent orange. The other man studied this staff through a transit, and moved the man like a puppet with subtle motions of his hand.

The quiet gave Dolph hope. Without the machinery noise the project seemed far less ominous. Dolph let the men work uninterrupted for as long as it took him to load and light his pipe. Russell beat upon a felled tree with a stick.

"I wondered when you would be back," Dolph said.

The man did not remove his eye from the transit, but pushed the other man back two steps with a flick of his hand.

"This cul-de-sac went in three years ago," Dolph said. "I expected the houses to follow—but then someone ran out of money, am I right?"

The man stayed at his work and Dolph considered upbraiding him for his rudeness. But he remained patient. Perhaps the man's mind was filled with calculations of distance and angle, and to utter a word would whisk them away irretrievably. Dolph went and lowered himself onto the tree his grandson pummeled. It was comfortable beneath him, a bit cool, but he crossed his legs, smoked, and waited.

A period of time passed in the cold and silence. Dolph spent it in reverie, of how the woods reminded him of his childhood, and of his early love for Elle, when she was young. In his daydream he lost track of Russell and an ingrained fear roused him. The boy was out of sight. Dolph whirled awkwardly and the boy was behind him, raptly bashing a leaf.

"Mr. Hjurak?" the man with the transit said. He pronounced the name incorrectly, sounding the "H," making an extra syllable of it. The chainsaw started again. Dolph felt he had risen from a deep sleep that aged him. His neck hurt from craning to look for Russell. The saw as it bit into another tree caused Russell to clutch Dolph's finger, and this small gesture of fear confirmed Dolph's belief that the day's events portended a bad turn.

His father was asleep when Carl came home from school. Dolph slept on a couch that had held the same ground for twice the length of Carl's life. Elle took the cushions outdoors every spring and beat on them with an unstrung tennis racket Dolph had salvaged in his wanderings. Now he slept with his back bowed out to the room, a light blanket spread over him. Russell sat on the floor at Dolph's feet, eating animal crackers and watching cartoons on TV with the sound low.

"Eight parcels, he says," Elle told Carl.

"Eight?"

"Eight *fancy* houses," Elle reported with the gravity of a radio newsman.

Carl tried to imagine eight houses on the cul-de-sac but could picture only the trees now standing there.

"The fancy houses won't have much land," he said.

"About that I wouldn't know," she said. Elle was preparing dinner; a potato in one hand, a peeler in the other.

"Did they say when they start work?"

"When? Already they've started," she said. "Already they have cut down a small forest of trees. When the ground is warm they dig the holes for the basements."

Dolph grumbled and stirred in his sleep. The blanket slid

off him and covered Russell's head. The boy picked the blanket off and let it drop. Elle put it back over her husband.

"What is going to happen is a mystery to him," she said. "That is the worst thing. The man knew his name, but he said it wrong. About the dogs he asked. Do they bark at night?"

"Ha," said Carl.

"And to his answers he didn't listen," she said. "The noise. The saw. The man looked at his papers. Your father he paid no attention to. Just the dogs. Do they bark? But to your father he didn't listen."

"They don't have to listen," Carl said. He changed into his coveralls and went outside to work on his cars in what little light remained. The feeling in the cold air was different in the direction of the woods; it seemed more unrestrained, yet fragile. He was flabbergasted by the work the men and the saw had done. A surprisingly neat, square canyon had been cut out of the trees, with only a scant picket left standing along their property line. This indicated to Carl that the first house would go up on the lot closest to them. He thought that was best; his father would only worry, waiting as the houses were built closer and closer to him. With the first house next to them, the worst would be over.

He turned back toward his own house, which squatted small and white in the moonlight. Ramshackle and in need of painting, bedecked with the sorry string of Christmas lights, the air of busy dereliction about the yard with his cars and the pen of dogs, his home for a long moment filled him with shame. For the first time, he realized that to the people who bought the new houses his family and their home would be an eyesore.

He touched the ground and it was reassuringly hard. They would not be going into it soon to begin the foundation. But, as Dolph had sensed, there existed the inexorable back-pressure of money behind the project, and the following day a sputtering yellow bulldozer arrived almost at dawn to clear the plot. The machine pushed the cut trees and stumps into high, ragged piles near the road, and on a later day yet another team of men with a pincer-crane and dump trucks went to work hauling the piles away. By the first of March the lot was nearly smooth. The rear line of trees remained like a buffer between the new ground and the Hjuraks' property.

"Our new neighbors think they won't be able to see us through those trees," Dolph said one evening. Elle was doing the dishes, letting the hot rinse water wash leisurely over her hands. The heat eased the aches that came and went in her knuckles.

"Let's go for a walk," he said.

"I have work to do."

"The dishes will still be dirty when we come back," he said. "This beautiful evening will be gone forever."

But she didn't want to go, and not only because she enjoyed doing the dishes. She knew they would walk only as far as the new lot and there Dolph would light his pipe and begin to stew about the coming of the neighbors.

She had watched him hurry to the window the previous Sunday when a car stopped in the cul-de-sac and two men and two women emerged. Dolph watched, muttering, while the people talked and made broad gestures out over the cleared space, and consulted a sheet of blue paper that unfolded to the dimensions of a bath towel. Finally they departed and Dolph said, glowering: "That was them. They looked young and rich." His envy saddened her.

"Come. Now," he said, tugging at her wet forearm.

"No. Beautiful evenings I've had enough of. But a dirty plate—that I understand."

Dolph went out, setting off the dogs. The evening light had gone past its point of delineating clarity and turned murky. He walked purposefully through that mocking line of trees and into the center of the clearing. He always was impressed how thoroughly the land had been scraped clean. The smooth earth, the walls of trees on three sides, all of it made Dolph feel he was standing on a bare stage.

Something about the visit of those four people had bothered him much more than the invasion of the clearing machinery. The people had been young, they had money. He had expected that. But as they looked over their blueprint and pointed to each spot in the clearing—where the study would be, what view the windows would command—he kept waiting for them to acknowledge at least with a glance or gesture his existence, and they never did. They did not appear to see his house. He and his family did not exist to them.

With little fanfare but the pop of the bulldozer's engine, the basement was dug. Another relay of dump trucks arrived to carry away the dirt from the hole. The dimensions of the basement startled Dolph. The side nearest his house reached to within forty feet of his property line. The house would be large, with virtually no back yard.

Dolph and Carl stood on the edge of the pit after the workmen had gone home.

"Foundation's next," Carl said.

"I hope so. It seems early for the roof."

His son grasped him by the shoulders and pretended to be about to push him in. Dolph found the instant of fear, of imbalance on the edge of the hole, to be exhilarating.

Carl walked around, kicking in stones and clods of dirt. At a point opposite to where his father stood he knelt and worked loose a fleck of bluish stone protruding from the basement wall.

"Hey!" he shouted, displaying an arrowhead between his thumb and forefinger, but when he looked up his father was urinating into the hole, a big grin on his face, and checking back over his shoulder to be sure he wasn't observed.

"Water in the basement," Dolph said. "Too bad."

Toward the end of March he took a bus to visit his daughters and do their income-tax returns. He arrived at noon and they were waiting at Margrithe's apartment, each of them with her little bundles of receipts from the previous year. The trip was a tradition, but also an annoyance. Out of three husbands, couldn't one of them figure out a tax return? As he straightened out their affairs and tried to finagle a small refund for each of them, he listened to their complaints about the lack of anything good on TV, about their husbands, about unwanted weight. He grew impatient and had to be careful to take the time to do their returns properly. He thought of Russell forced to spend the day without him, and Elle's solution to the boy's slightest hint of restlessness: feed him. That same strategy had backfired in the wide butts and grumpy faces of his daughters. He was finished at four o'clock, kissed them all goodbye, and walked the six blocks to the bus. Margrithe wanted him to stay for dinner but he didn't have the courage. "Don't forget to sign the returns," he said. He suspected at least one of the couples would forget. They had before.

In his absence, Elle reported, more men had come and cut down trees on another of the cul-de-sac lots. Work also had progressed on the new house. The forms for the foundation had gone in.

"Tomorrow the cement arrives, Carl was told," Elle said. "Cole is the name of the people who will be living next door. By Halloween they hope to move in. At the latest Thanksgiving. The woman, she's a lawyer. The man, he pushes papers. According to Carl."

Dolph scratched his jaw, yawned, and asked, "How was my Russell today?"

"Russell was Russell," Elle said.

"Is he fat yet?"

"Fat he isn't," she said. She knew Dolph thought she spoiled the child with food, but the rich snacks and abundant meals she prepared were simply tokens of love. She was proudest of her cooking: she was most content when assuaging a hunger. Russell's appetite was immense and she joked with him that when he opened his mouth to eat she saw the glow of his furnace burning at the end of a dark coal-chute.

"Did he ask for me?"

"All day," she exaggerated. "Every five minutes he asked for his Papa."

"Thank you," Dolph said, and kissed her cheek.

"Dinner soon."

"I'm going next door."

The foundation forms were splashed white with dry cement. The forms hinted at walls, which in turn hinted at neighbors—strangers—occupying that space. Dolph wondered if he would ever be comfortable with that idea.

Many years before, he had put up a new mailbox at the end of the driveway. After digging the post hole, and before pouring the cement, he placed one of Elle's rings at the bottom of the hole. The ring held in place beneath the cement all that time made him feel rooted to that generous piece of land, and to that dilapidated house he had once considered merely a point of departure. When Elle remarked about a ring she had misplaced he proudly told her what he had done. She didn't understand and was angry for three days. She saw only that he had buried a cherished ring—a gift from him, as a matter of fact—without asking her permission. He tried to explain and she said, "My ring you had to use? Why not your favorite spoon? Or one of the children's blocks?"

Now he stood at the edge of the basement pit and took a pipe from his pocket. The pipe was old and recently retired from active use. The bowl was crisply stained blood-brown and the sweet smell of tobacco had turned bitter. The pipe nevertheless possessed a single, extended aura of the pleasure it had provided for Dolph as he smoked it. He was not parting cavalierly with the pipe. He sucked through the stem one last time, spat with some distaste, then lobbed the pipe underhand into the moat of the foundation forms. In the morning the cement would be poured;

it would harden, and the house would rise on that solid base. Regardless of what happened with the new neighbors, that small particle from his life would be a part of theirs. This gave him hope they might be friends.

The house grew up through the summer like a plant, with green tints in the wood, the glass, and the shade the house cast. The other lots on the cul-de-sac underwent the changes necessary for building upon them. Good weather brought with it a tumult of power tools and ringing hammers. Dolph sat in a chair in his back yard. He fanned himself and smoked. Or he drank iced tea. The design of the new house was a surprise to him. The primary feature of its southern exposure, the side facing Dolph's property, was a two-story-high wall of glass that revealed the hollow airy spaces still being constructed by the carpenters. The shape and dimensions of the house spoke of great expense. Yet the house was situated on a lot so small he sometimes felt he could reach out from his chair and run a finger down all that glass.

Kevin came to get Russell that evening. He joined Dolph in the back yard. Elle provided beer and a plate of celery stuffed with cream cheese, this ringed by crackers in the shape of bells.

"Tell your secrets while you can," Dolph said. "Pretty soon they'll hear everything we say."

"It does sort of *loom*," Kevin said.

"It worries me."

"A house?" Kevin said.

"Yes. Other things, too."

"Nothing to worry about, Dad. Hey . . . did I tell you? There's a girl I want you to meet."

"I have a girl."

"Her name's Lorraine," Kevin said. "I like her."

"What do you like about her?"

"She's gorgeous. She's a data processor. She's been divorced for two years."

"How many kids does she have?" Dolph asked.

"Two boys and a girl."

"Bring her to dinner. Don't do anything rash."

"What does that mean?"

"Russell needs a mother," Dolph said.

"He has Mom."

"He needs someone of his own."

"Lorraine likes him," Kevin said.

"What's not to like? But she's got three who'll come ahead of him. Russell shouldn't finish fourth to anyone," Dolph said.

Kevin took Russell home soon after.

An unfamiliar sound came from the front yard later that evening. Dolph went outside. Carl stood wiping his hands on a rag and grinning. The sound was produced by the unmuffled engine of a 1972 Buick. It was so loud Dolph couldn't hear the dogs, but saw them roiling in the shadows. Carl switched off the ignition and the sound of the dogs came up like a TV.

"You got one running," Dolph said. "I salute you. What about the rest of them?"

"They're coming along," Carl nodded. "One needs a distributor and a new radiator. Another needs a starter. Another a clutch. This one here needs a muffler and a reverse gear."

"You can start it," Dolph said, "but you can't back it out of here?"

"Right," Carl said. He unplugged his work light and wound up the cord, using his elbow and the base of his thumb as guides. His eyes were on the new house.

"Want to go in there?" he asked.

"Inside?"

"I found a way in."

"You're breaking into houses?"

"Exploring," he said. They crossed the yard. House frames

had gone up on two of the lots. Another lot had the foundation poured, another just the trees cleared off. Each development made the neighborhood seem more alien to Dolph; how long before he was used to the change in the light, before he forgot what life had been like living next to the woods?

Carl picked a key off the ledge above the front door. "So obvious," he said.

The air inside the house was cool and smelled of plaster dust and wood. None of the rooms had a finished look. Scraps of lumber and ruined nails lay where they had been dropped. The plumbing in the kitchen was exposed and none of the counters or appliances were in. Dolph was disappointed; he thought he had been closer to meeting his new neighbors.

"Up here," Carl said. They took a stairway to a loft that overlooked the house's showcase room. To the right was a two-story stone fireplace still in progress; to the left was a wet bar and sunken dining area. Straight ahead was the wall of glass. From where Dolph stood he thought he could jump onto his roof, so close it appeared.

A light went on in his bathroom. Elle came into the light, visible to him from her shoulders up. He watched her undress and drop her nightgown down over her. After she washed her face she studied herself in the mirror with more intentness and interest than Dolph thought her capable of. Her hair was bound up clear of the water; the style always had appealed to him, accentuating as it did the strong planes of her face, though they were softening now. She shut off the light. He would have to put up curtains.

"Ready?" Carl asked.

Dolph was embarrassed, wondering if his son had watched Elle wash and gaze into the mirror.

"Ready, Dad?"

Dolph nodded, but he didn't turn away.

"Come on, Dad," Carl said, and touched his father's arm.

"What is that?" Dolph pointed. "That dark spot on the roof."

Carl looked along his father's finger.

"I don't see anything."

"Right there," Dolph said.

"It's dark, Dad. You can check in the morning. My guess is it'll still be there."

They went back down the stairs and out the front door. Elle served them cinnamon cake and coffee. She had let her hair down again and with a bemused little smile she honored Dolph's request that she pin it back up off her neck, and when he ardently kissed that spot in the quiet of their room he felt her breathing race as in the old days.

A dog got loose the next morning and the dark spot on the roof was forgotten in the excitement of the chase. Rex was the dog's name. A large, unruly dog, he timed his excited lunge at the pen door just right, catching Carl with the latch undone and his weight unbalanced by the fifty-pound food bag he carried on his shoulder. Carl went over backward. Rex ran into the yard and stopped. His first steps of freedom were tentative. He sniffed the tire on one of Carl's cars. Then he looked back at Carl, who had relocked the pen and now approached with a palmful of dog chow as bait. In an instant Rex was in full stride, across the yard, around the house, and out of sight.

Carl got Dolph and they gave chase in the direction Rex had been heading. Only by the purest luck did they catch a glimpse of the dog already a half-mile from home. By the time they got turned around, Rex had lost them again.

"He hasn't eaten since yesterday," Dolph said. "He'll be back in an hour."

But Rex was never seen again.

"Worthless animal," Dolph said later.

"Do we need the dogs at all?" Elle asked. She was warm from the oven, where her biscuits were cooking. "Hunting you don't go anymore. One would do for a watchdog. Why a pack?"

"Why did we need so many kids?" Dolph said. "A boy, a girl, then stop, I said. No. We had to have more children."

"Silliness," Elle said, turning away.

"The kids I liked. The dogs I like, too. That's why."

"Nobody dragged you into bed all those nights."

"Hush!" Dolph said, with a shocked grin, his eyes darting to Russell, who paid no attention.

"The children, they grow up and move away to lives of their own," Elle said. "Forever we've had these dogs."

"In my old age the dogs are the comfort to me my children aren't," Dolph said.

"Comfort," she mocked. "Feed them you don't. Play with them you don't. Curse them when they bark, that is all you do."

Coming in that evening, Carl reported, "They're very restless. They don't understand what's happened to Rex. But they understand he's not in the pen with them anymore. I think they're intrigued by that."

"A prison break, you say they're plotting?" Dolph teased.

"They aren't eating."

"For that we should say a prayer of thanks. Dogs that don't eat. Hallelujah!"

The new neighbors came in a September downpour to move some smaller items into their house. Lamps, bookshelves, a three-legged stool, plants in clay pots, cartons a woman could carry. Friends helped. They all seemed to be the same age, Dolph observed; roughly Kevin's age. Dolph watched at his window. He hadn't been in the new house since Carl had taken him there. He was reminded of the dark circle on the roof; would it still be there? The rain fell too hard at present for him to check.

The neighbors made a number of trips in varying configurations of people. Someone always stayed behind, usually a petite woman with short black hair. She directed the movers. Dolph saw her standing with one arm pointing, then changing her mind and pointing the other way, her other hand scratching her chin in indecision. When Dolph thought they all had left and the house was empty again, she surprised him passing in front of a window or standing at the back door and smoking a cigarette. Watching his house. He shrank back.

Toward nightfall the work ceased. The rain had let up. A dinner of something and beer was served on the floor of the room with all the glass, the people sitting like Indians and eating off boxes, and laughing. Around midnight everyone went away. A light was left burning in an upstairs room, and that was what saddened Dolph most of all: the presence of light in the house made the theft of his privacy complete.

He hadn't thought the house was ready to be occupied. Two weeks ago he had looked in the windows and at that time he saw countless small tasks needing to be done. But the neighbors had begun to shift the weight of their existence, each possession like a stone holding down the lines of a tent. They had eaten under the roof and illuminated the house against darkness. It nearly was home.

Hoping to see what was on his roof, Dolph went outside. The dogs made a fuss until he hushed them. The late hour was exciting; ordinarily he was long asleep by midnight, but the procession of movement next door left him alert and protective of his property. The night was too dark for him to see what was on his roof, though he backed into the neighbors' muddy yard to get a glimpse.

Everything was quiet and orderly. Brushing against a tree had wet his hand and he wiped it on his pants. He knocked out his pipe against his palm, and refilled the bowl. His boots were heavy with mud. That would be the hardest part of making the new house feel like home: growing the grass to a point where it seemed rooted, where a child could safely roll on it.

He went to a window and looked in. A scattering of cartons was on the floor. The wires for a light fixture snaked out of the ceiling. He turned the corner of the house and went along the wall of glass. With his face pressed close to see inside, he discovered a man and a woman on the floor in the dark. The wom-

an's back was to him and it gleamed in her exertion. She blocked
the man's vision as she straddled him. A green beer-bottle was
lying on its side next to them. Dolph took a step back, then
another. He stood for a long time and just watched with a clinical
sort of envy: that they were young, that they had the money to
rob him of his privacy, that they were in there while he stood
in the damp chill unable to sleep. The neighbors did not slow
or break apart or twist to shame him with a stare, and all at once
the woman seemed to snap in half and collapse onto the man's
chest, where his arms enfolded her. In the stillness that followed,
Dolph made his escape.

The neighbors took over their new house by degrees and
Dolph suspected they stayed some nights and not others. He
watched for signs of children—toys, a bike, a swing set—and
saw none. If there were children, he would have a hope of becoming their friend, and of finding his way through them to their
parents.

A stack of redwood lumber was delivered to the rear of the
lot. Its presence spooked Dolph, for he prided himself on being
attuned to everything about his neighbors, yet he heard no truck
or crane or clatter of wood. The lumber simply was there when
he awakened.

A carpenter Dolph had never seen before came to work on
the wood. He set up two horses and laid a board across them.
With a yellow tape he measured the wood and made small nicks
with a pencil. He made quick, efficient cuts with a power saw
whose high-pitched noise upset the dogs. Dolph let the man work
for an hour before approaching. In that time of careful observation the nature of the project became apparent: a fence was
being built.

Dolph introduced himself. The carpenter said his name was
Marion.

"They aren't in the house all the way and already they're
building fences," Dolph said.

The carpenter looked up from his work and shrugged.

"They going all the way around?"

"No," Marion said. "Just the rear lot line."

"How high?"

"Ten feet."

"All that glass on the south side—then a ten-foot fence?" Dolph said. "It'll block the sun. Their yard's so small."

Marion went on working. Dolph stood without moving, without saying a word. In time he returned to his house to monitor the work from the window, but when the first post hole was being dug he came outside again.

"Stop," he said, a hand raised. "That's my property you're digging on."

The carpenter pursed his lips. The hole was on Dolph's side of the line of trees left standing at the rear of the neighbor's lot.

"I'm afraid you're mistaken, Mr. Hjurak," Marion said. "See those stakes?" He pointed to a small stick of white wood—a small orange flag flying from it—out by the road, and another like it sunk in the ground a distance to Dolph's right. "Run a line between those two stakes and that's the south boundary of their property. The trees are on their lot."

"If they wanted privacy, why build a huge house on a tiny lot?" Dolph asked.

"I can't speak for them."

"This is a beautiful house. But it's wasted here."

"I don't know."

"They cut down all the trees," Dolph said.

The carpenter flicked on his saw. All afternoon the racket he made flew across Dolph's property line to disrupt his composure. At dusk the woman came out of the house to inspect the work. She slapped the wood and the sound was solid. Dolph wondered if she had been at home all day.

"It will give Russell something to throw a ball against," Dolph said.

"That they would love—a cookout in the back yard of their

new home and knockknockknock the boy from next door is throwing a ball against their precious fence," Elle said.

"I would relish their discomfort."

"The fence they built. On their property it stands," Elle said. "Fences they need, let them put up fences."

Her anger surprised him; he thought she didn't care. He put his arms around her waist and kissed the damp nape of her neck, but she pushed him away with a sharp, backward thrust of her hips.

"Hot-blooded we are all of a sudden," she said. "Showing off? Afraid you'll lose me to the man next door?"

"Maybe they need a cook."

Elle turned her back to him. "The travel time you couldn't beat," she said.

Toward the end of summer Kevin married his girlfriend, Lorraine. The four children and Lorraine's sister were the only guests, and then the sister had to go to work. The wedding party went on to Dolph's. Kevin pushed the doorbell, but remembered it hadn't worked since his sophomore year in high school. He pounded on the door. Dolph was asleep on the couch, Elle was in the kitchen, Carl was taking a bath. Kevin knocked. He had hoped his family would be awake and alert, possibly even dressed. They would slap him on the back, shake his hand, kiss him, kiss his wife.

He heard someone scratching at the inside of the door.

"Dad? Open up!"

Dolph pulled the door open. There was his beloved Russell in a crushed-velvet tux, fronting for a small mob of strangers, the one in the shadows at the rear vaguely familiar.

"We got married, Dad!" this man announced loudly. A woman stepped forward and kissed Dolph on the cheek. She was pretty, he saw, her eyes watery blue and begging for approval. Her clothes reeked of smoke.

"We should've invited you," the woman said. "Kevin wanted to surprise you."

"Surprised, Dad?"

Elle rescued Dolph. She steered him out of the doorway, unblocking the path for their son and his new family. The woman's three kids took the couch.

"Surprised, Dad?"

" 'Surprised' I think is a mild word," Elle said. "Come in. Come in. You must be hungry."

"This is Lorraine," Kevin said.

She and Elle exchanged false little kisses. "We should've invited you," Lorraine said. "I should've visited you so we could get to be friends."

"Don't trouble yourself," Elle said. She was as short as Lorraine, which pleased her. Kevin's first wife had been a tall, hard thing with a distracted and superior air. Elle also sensed in Lorraine's ample hips and breasts the same potential plumpness that settled so easily on her.

Dolph looked at the children who had taken over his couch, two boys together, the girl at one end, subtly removed from the entire gathering. Russell stood where he had stopped upon entering the house, just outside the bathroom door. Dolph went to him and plucked off the velvet bowtie, which had rubbed a red mark into the underside of Russell's jaw.

"Gotta go, Papa."

"Carl?" Dolph knocked. "Emergency."

In they barged. Carl's narrow face was smeared with soap. Water the color of new oil lapped to within an inch of the tub rim.

"Thanks, Dad," Carl said, his eyes shut.

"Hi, Uncle Carl."

"Hello, Russell. How're you doing?"

"Daddy got married today."

"Oh. Are they in here, too?"

"They're outside," Dolph whispered. "A *surprise*. I'll say.

Finish and come out as soon as you can. Tell me who Kevin's new wife reminds you of."

In the week before school started, Dolph watched over the three new kids, as well as Russell. The three kept to themselves, speaking only rarely. The girl did not talk to her brothers or to anyone else. The boys excluded Russell from their little huddles of consultation in the yard. The dogs frightened them. Dolph asked only that the children let him know where they were going to be. If asked, he could not have pinpointed any of the three at any particular time of day. Over the course of the week he didn't lose anyone, and considered himself a success. He was relieved when school started and Russell came alone in the morning.

The World Series was being played when Ronny—the oldest boy—first took notice of the redwood fence. Ten feet high, it ran from corner to corner across the rear of the new house's lot. Dolph had come to appreciate the fence. The privacy it afforded was nearly as complete as the woods. The top of the house was visible, but without the lure of all that glass to spy in, he often forgot anyone lived there.

In the cool twilight of October, in the last hour before nightfall preceding Game 3 of the Series, Kevin and his family paid a visit. They planned to eat dinner and watch the game. Ronny and his brother, Paul, slipped outside before dinner. Russell didn't ask to go along. The boys were gone an hour, and then Elle had Lorraine call them to eat. Mud was tracked in, and the boys apologized only after Dolph made a commotion. Elle shushed him for criticizing their guests, but his outburst soured the meal.

Kevin only relaxed when the game came on and he had taken his customary place on the floor, a pillow propped behind his head against the couch. He looked so familiar to Dolph stretched out there; a beer in hand, his arm around his son, who had fallen asleep. Dolph had to bring a kitchen chair into the crowded room, the three kids having grabbed the couch (though the girl, whose name was Kim, did homework all evening). Lorraine stayed in the kitchen with Elle. Carl floated: watching the game from the doorway, reading the paper at the kitchen table, running a grinder in his workroom until Kevin complained about the noise and the snow in the TV picture. Elle brought out beer and pop and a tray of carrots, celery sticks, and cauliflower, and a small brown crock of warm cheese. Dolph heard her talking to Lorraine. Their voices seemed nervous and strained to him as they came in from the kitchen. He noticed that when a silence extended beyond a half-minute Elle came out where the game was being played to check on drinks and food, and to hover at a loss rather than go back in with her new daughter-in-law.

The boys in their time outside had painted the number 343 on the redwood fence. Dolph discovered it in the morning. The first 3 was slightly larger than the other two digits. The hour was early; he phoned Kevin's, but nobody answered. His son, Lorraine, and the four kids had departed within seconds of the final out the night before, an evacuation that had the haste and impatience of a fire drill.

Dolph could not explain to himself the significance of the 343. Was it some sort of gang code? He had read in the paper how gangs marked their turf with just that sort of sign, comprehensible only to those who would care about its presence.

"What if the neighbors see it?" he asked Elle. "Their new fence!"

"So clean it off," she said.

"Those little hoods will clean it off!"

"Do they care? No. They wouldn't have done it if they cared."

"I'll tell them to clean it off."

"Tell them whatever you want," Elle said. "But clean it off they won't. Who's to make them? You? Their mother? Kevin? Hah! None of you."

He bought a jug of turpentine and a small can of redwood stain, but when he invited Kevin and his family over they had made other arrangements for the evening's entertainment. Dolph didn't mention the number.

The following day he came home in the afternoon and Ronny and Paul were there in the front yard. Each wore a baseball glove.

"Where's your dad?"

"Mom divorced him," Ronny said.

For an instant, Dolph's heart dropped, that Kevin could kill a marriage so quickly, but then he realized the boy was speaking of his real father, long gone. He wondered what—if anything —Kevin meant to these kids.

Ronny threw a ball in a high, careful arc toward the fence, and as Paul ran back to catch it Dolph understood immediately the 343. It was a distance mark; a small bit of detail the boys had added to their game. Dolph knew that a kid—using just that stretch of fence and that sloppy white number—could create an entire stadium in his imagination, and fill it with people. Paul touched the fence expertly without looking at it, his glove shading his eyes. The sky was dim, a high blue, and darkening fast. He caught the ball one-handed with his back to the fence. For the first time since he'd met them, Dolph liked the boys.

"What happens when the ball goes over?"

"We go around and get it."

"Have they said anything to you?"

"We haven't seen anybody," Ronny said.

The boys called Dolph from inside when darkness was nearly upon them, claiming the ball had hit the very top of the fence and caromed onto Dolph's roof, becoming stuck in the gutter.

The dogs set up an enthusiastic howl as he carried a stepladder past them. He found the ball right away and tossed it down to the boys, who went inside without saying a word. Dolph was glad they left. He took a precarious seat atop the ladder and lit his pipe. Movement—interruptions in the path of lights— could be detected in the house next door.

Elle came outside and called to him. They were out of sight of each other. He liked the sound of her voice, the weight of concern for him.

"Dolph? Are you out here? A phone call for you."

He turned carefully on the ladder, feeling a little dizzy, and then his eye caught sight of the dark spot on the roof. It was a hat, too far up for him to reach. The hat's origin was a mystery. Only on the coldest days did Dolph wear a hat. Certainly he never threw one onto his roof.

The two boys were on the couch eating pretzels and dip, and sucking bottles of red pop.

"Who are our guests?" he asked.

"The phone," Elle whispered.

"Where's Kevin? And Russell?"

"Answer the phone, please."

He held the phone against his stomach. "A hat is on our roof," he said. "Do you know how a hat got on our roof?"

"No. Talk."

"Hello," he said.

"Mr. Hjurak?"

"Yes."

"My name is Lydia Cole. My husband and I built the house that adjoins your property to the north."

"Yes," Dolph said. "A beautiful house."

"Thank you."

"But that fence. Why block the sun with that fence?"

"That was an aesthetic decision," she said. "But that's not the reason I called."

Dolph waited; he felt safe, having been complimentary. They could not accuse him of being impolite.

"We were wondering if you could do something about your dogs," she said.

"*Do* something?"

"They're extremely noisy, Mr. Hjurak," she said. He noted

how her voice had cooled just the degree his had heated. She was a lawyer, he'd been told. Her husband pushed papers, and he had let her make the call.

"They're watchdogs," Dolph said. "Crime is not unheard of in this neighborhood."

"You need seven watchdogs?"

"You've counted them?"

"Yes."

"You've been in my yard?" he asked.

"My husband counted them from the road."

"He couldn't. From the road he could only see dogs milling about. But seven? Or seventy? He couldn't tell from the road."

"That isn't the point, Mr. Hjurak." She said nothing for a moment. He wished her face was before him; he'd seen her without clothes, but he'd never had a good look at her face.

"Our builder reported that you frequently were on our property in the course of the house's construction," she said. "Trespassing charges seem like a moot point, don't you agree? Now—as to the dogs—I merely wanted to discuss them with you as neighbors. Who hopefully will be good neighbors for many years to come."

"If I get rid of my dogs," Dolph said.

"I didn't ask you to do that."

"But it's what you wanted."

"To be honest, I'd be delighted if you got rid of your dogs. But"—she added quickly—"all I'm asking is that you bring them under some sort of control. Every car that passes, every time you open your door, every time *we* open *our* door—your dogs bark. We moved here from the city to get away from that kind of tension-inducing noise."

"In the winter—when the houses are closed up—it's not so bad," Dolph said.

"All our windows are shut now, Mr. Hjurak. But your dogs sound like they're in the same room with us," she said.

"I can't bring them indoors. There's barely room for us."

"I'll leave it to you," she said. "I know you'll treat our concerns with the same respect we'd accord yours."

Elle massaged his shoulders while he sat at the kitchen table and fumed.

"That fence! How neighborly is that fence?"

"Not at all," Elle said. She squeezed his neck affectionately. Carl washed his hands and sat down. Elle set food on the table. The sight of it, the smell of it, made Dolph feel better.

"What about them?" he asked, pointing to the boys.

"They already ate."

"Here?"

"Does it matter?" Elle asked. "Eat."

"I'm not getting rid of those dogs," Dolph said. "Not *one*."

"Eat. She's a troublemaker."

"They *are* pretty noisy," Carl said.

"A traitor in my house," Dolph said. "The man who feeds them, who is most loved by them. A traitor."

"Relax, Dad. Will you? We really only need Taffy. The rest just eat and bark."

Elle touched her husband's rough cheek. "Bark they do," she said.

"And what would I do with the others?"

"You can always find a home for a good dog," Carl said.

"Your decision," Dolph said, pointing to his son. "I wash my hands of it."

His secret hope was that the dogs would remain, and in the muffled cold of winter the neighbors' hearing would be less acute. By the weekend, however, two dogs were gone.

"What, did you just take them out and turn them loose?" he asked Carl.

"They'd come back if I did that."

"Rex didn't."

"He escaped, remember?"

"Well, what then?" Dolph asked.

"You washed your hands."

"I didn't think you'd just make them disappear."

"I took Thor and Georgy—the two loudest," Carl said. "Maybe our new neighbors will be satisfied with the reduction in noise."

"Are they dead on some roadside?"

"No."

A sunny day in January, Dolph was shoveling the driveway and stopped at the commencement of an ache in his chest. The blade of the shovel was red plastic, and seemed to glow. The snow was dry and effervescent. He stood for fifteen minutes just breathing very slowly. The work was nearly done, the effort was keeping him warm. He looked forward to a nap.

A car stopped in the road and a woman got out. Only when she spoke did Dolph realize who she was.

"Mr. Hjurak, can I ask you what you intend to do about those dogs?"

She was a very pretty woman, he was somehow pleased to see, with a red tip of cold to her nose. The air made her eyes water. He felt stronger than her, felt that the cold had less of a hold on him.

"You can ask," Dolph said.

"I'm asking."

"My son got rid of two of them. The two loudest."

"The two loudest?" she said. "Every night since I first spoke with you my husband and I have had our sleep disrupted by your dogs."

"You must be light sleepers."

"That's not the point," she said.

"Talk to Carl," Dolph said. "My son. I gave him the responsibility."

"There are noise-pollution laws, Mr. Hjurak," she said.

"Dogs barking is noise pollution?"

"Any noise that is uncomfortable, dis—— What is that on our fence?"

She struck off through the snow and immediately Dolph felt like a child caught in the act of a misdeed. The 343 still gleamed where the boys had painted it. Faded some in three months, but not much. He was going to have Ronny and Paul remove it, but then the woman called with her complaint about the dogs and after he hung up he had decided to let it ride.

"You've *defaced* our property," she said. She smudged white paint onto a finger of her glove. "What's the meaning of this?"

"My son's stepkids did that last fall," he said. "They were pretending your fence was a baseball stadium. That's the distance from home plate—343 feet."

"And when do you intend to remove it?"

"Spring."

"*Spring?*"

"Nobody's noticed it," Dolph said. "*You* haven't noticed it and it's been there since October."

"I come and go from the other direction," she said.

"In the spring I'll remove the numbers *and* restain your fence. I promise."

"I can't live the rest of the winter with a vandalized fence," she said.

"There's nothing I can do until the weather gets warm," Dolph said, and this was a comfort to him.

He loved his little house in the wintertime, when the windows were snug with frost and the furnace turned over with a soft click and warm blasts from the vents.

"The woman complained about the dogs today," he said.

"How can she hear them?" Carl asked. "I don't hear them."

"You aren't listening for them," Elle said.

"You got rid of two," Dolph said. "What are the chances of getting rid of some more?"

"Before, you washed your hands of it," Carl said.

"She saw the 343. She knows we—someone in our family —vandalized her fence. She talked about noise-pollution laws. She could make trouble."

"Ignore her," Elle said.

"I'm telling you what she told me."

Saturday followed and in the morning Dolph was drawn to the window by an uproar of dogs. Carl had a car running and as Dolph watched he led two dogs from the pen. Their attitudes were of boundless elation and curiosity. They leaped to lick Carl's face, and as they danced in the deep snow their long tongues flopped in the cold air like wet, steaming socks. Carl tied their leashes to the back-door armrests. Dolph heard their happy barks even through the car's closed door, through the thin walls of his house. Carl was gone most of the day and returned alone.

"I found them good homes," he said.

"Don't tell me," Dolph said.

With only three dogs out back, Dolph felt exposed to the whims of criminals. The dogs barked as frequently, but without the orchestral warning seriousness of the pack. Many nights he took his place in bed alongside Elle before it occurred to him that he hadn't heard the dogs all night. He rose and went to the back door, made noise opening the locks, so that he would hear Taffy and the other two stir and bark softly as if clearing their throats, waiting for whatever was to follow. Thus reassured of their vigilance, Dolph went back to bed.

Yet in the spring the woman called to him over the top of her fence. She held a pair of pruning shears.

"Did you have a nice winter, Mr. Hjurak?"

"Very nice. And you?"

"We heard your dogs last night."

"Did you?"

"A little past midnight. I remember the time because I made a point of looking at the clock beside the bed. The red numbers glow in the dark."

"We have only three dogs now. That's down from seven."

"Did you know there's a hat on your roof?" she asked.

"Yes," Dolph said, though he had forgotten. "Every day I see a million things I've got to do. I start on one, think of something else, start on it. Nothing is ever finished. That's why that hat is still on my roof."

"I make a list," she said. "Then I prioritize the list and start with the job that is most important. If I think of something else I have to do, I see where it fits on the list and I put it there."

"We've gotten rid of four dogs," Dolph said. "I think that goes way beyond being neighborly."

"I can't see from here. Is that number gone?"

"Not yet. It will be. Winter's barely over."

"My husband's the one who hates your dogs," she said. "He's an extremely poor sleeper. Near insomniac. He's also under a great deal of stress at work. He needs what little sleep he can get."

"I'm sorry," Dolph said. "But I won't get rid of any more dogs."

"Three dogs?"

"Taffy, Butch, and Max. The best-behaved dogs of the bunch," he said.

"And what happened to the others?"

"My son took them away. I didn't want to know what became of them."

"He didn't have them put to sleep, did he?" she asked.

"I don't know," Dolph said. "Would that bother you? They'd be very quiet then."

"Don't take this lightly," she said.

"I wouldn't dare."

"And clean off that number." She disappeared behind the fence.

He wanted Ronny and Paul to help with the eradication of the 343, but the kids didn't come around much lately. There was no lesson to be learned if he did the job himself, but finally he felt he couldn't wait.

"Where are those two?" he asked.

"They have other lives," Elle said. Agitated about something, she kept wiping the same spotless section of kitchen table.

"Tell me what you know," Dolph said.

"Kevin calls. He talks. He worries." She shrugged.

"He can't talk to me?"

"He's embarrassed."

"Is it the boys?"

"The boys are part of his worries," Elle said. "He calls Ronny the troublemaker. Down his marks have gone. Out all night he stays. Drugs, Kevin says, the one you smoke. Ronny has been caught selling the drug to kids at school. Younger kids."

"Oh, Lord."

"Yes."

"All right, he's a bad apple," Dolph said. "But he's not Kevin's kid. Russell—a perfect boy. *He* is Kevin's kid."

"A father is what he wants to be for those other three," Elle said. "Ronny—Kevin tells me—scorns him. Kim, no one knows what goes on in her head. Paul, Kevin thinks, is still making up his mind."

"Worry about Russell. Tell him that when he talks to you. Let the lost causes be lost," Dolph said.

"And Lorraine. Kevin says they aren't happy. He used a word. 'Deliriously.' They aren't deliriously happy."

Dolph tried to count the months his son and the woman had been married. Too brief a time, regardless. He remembered Kevin lying on the floor watching TV while his new bride tried to make small talk in the kitchen. He'd looked like a kid then.

" 'Promise you won't tell Dad,' he said," Elle remarked. "He's so afraid of doing something foolish in front of you."

"All right. I'll play dumb."

In the dark he brushed the thinner over the 343. Green light from the neighbors' house poured over the top of the fence and leaked in slices through the narrow gaps between the boards. He heard music. The neighbors' back yard was filled with voices, laughter, little flirtatious shrieks. As he spread the thinner the number receded into the shadows of the wood until only a milky cloud remained. In the morning the party was over and the mark on the fence was easier to see. Dolph was up early. He'd had trouble sleeping; the dogs were one reason, but also the music, laughter, the voices. He kept listening for them, trying to understand them, and the effort kept him awake. At 4:00 a.m. he'd taken the phone and let it hum in his lap while he debated calling the police, and decided the complaint would be too obviously petty. He felt better having resisted the urge to be vindictive and fell asleep soon afterward.

Now he held a small can of redwood stain and dipped a new brush into it, then painted the stain in long strokes over the milky spot on the fence. Squinting, he could still see the 343. If he was interested in doing the job properly he would have to stain the entire fence to achieve an evenness of coat. But he wouldn't do that. When the stain dried it would blend well enough.

That finished, Dolph carried a ladder and rake to the side of the house nearest the fence. He climbed the ladder and reached with the rake to snag the mystery hat off the roof. The hat practically dissolved, so rotted was it from the sun and rain. He looked in the band for a name. Nothing was to be found there.

Retrieving the hat also had been an excuse to elevate himself above the fence. The laughter and clatter and the music of the party had made his desire to spy very nearly a lust the night before. He associated the party with an experience, a way of life, forever lost to him. Now he would permit himself to look in on the aftermath.

Beyond a mild rumpling of the back yard—glasses lying tipped in the grass, the sparkle of something shattered on the patio, Chinese lanterns pulled low with the night's moisture—there was little about the yard to indicate a party had taken place.

But at the end of the patio farthest from Dolph, on a narrow chaise longue, somebody curled under a yellow blanket began to stir. A foot emerged daintily, as if being dipped into the air, and quickly withdrew. Dolph held his breath. The foot had been small, in a high-heeled sandal with the ankle strap unbuckled. Dolph sat on the top of the ladder. The green glass face of the house was impassive. He would have liked to smoke but feared the smell would tip off his presence. In that motionless way he sat for an hour, and only the yellow mound moved less than he did. At the end of the hour his front door opened, setting off an alarm of dogs, and Elle's high-pitched summoning voice called him in for breakfast. The yellow blanket shifted with an irritation he might have imagined. He waited ten more minutes and then went inside.

"Did you hear their party last night?"

"No," Elle said.

"How about you?"

"No," Carl said.

"They kept me awake."

"Call the cops," Carl said. "That'd be rich."

"I almost did. But I could only see that leading to trouble. She'd turn it to her advantage," Dolph said.

The dogs were extremely restless that night, going off at the slightest provocation, though the air was cool and still. Toward midnight one of them began to howl a mournful croon into the moonless sky.

"Jesus," Dolph, in bed, muttered. The noise had awakened him. Elle loomed beside, so quiet, so rhythmic in her breathing that he couldn't tell if she was awake or asleep. A second dog took up the song and they were so piercing they seemed to be shoulder to shoulder at the foot of the bed.

He wasn't surprised when the telephone rang. He had gotten out of bed and gone into the kitchen, and he answered the phone before the first ring was finished.

"Do you hear that?" she asked.

"Of course I hear it."

"What do you intend to do about it?"

"I was on my way out to tell them to shut up," Dolph said. "I don't intend to do anything else."

"Get rid of them, Mr. Hjurak. My husband is being driven mad by your dogs."

"Your party last night kept me awake," Dolph said. "I didn't call and harass you. I didn't ask—"

"*One* party? One rather sedate party? Compared to almost a year of howling dogs?"

Dolph sniffed. "I was kept awake."

She lowered her voice. "I'm sorry I keep harping on your dogs," she said. "But I don't know what else to do."

"I'll talk to my son," he said. "One dog's enough for me."

"Thank you, Mr. Hjurak. You have no idea what welcome news that is over here." She paused, and in the quiet Dolph heard a low voice in the room with her. She sounded distracted when she said, "Thank you again. I must go now. Good night."

He wore a jacket over his robe, left his shoes untied, and carried a flashlight. The howling trailed off when he unlocked the back door, and then the dogs began to bark.

He flicked the beam of light across the pen.

"Hush!" he said.

Butch and Max thrust their muzzles against the fence. They reached out to touch him and whimpered ecstatically when he drew close. Their breath was hot and wet on his hand. His light found Taffy in the rear of the pen. She was lying on her side, her eyes shut, a panting smile on her face. Five puppies squirmed in the canyon formed by her body and legs, and a sixth new dog was at that moment emerging.

ABOUT THE AUTHOR

Charles Dickinson is the author of two novels, *Waltz in Marathon* and *Crows*. His short stories have appeared in the *The New Yorker, Esquire, The Atlantic Monthly,* and *Grand Street,* and he is the 1984 winner of the O. Henry Award for "Risk," one of the eleven short stories included in *With or Without.* He lives with his wife and children in Palatine, Illinois.

Beattie, Ann. *Where You'll Find Me.*
$7.95 ISBN 0-02-016560-9

Carrère, Emmanuel. *The Mustache.*
$7.95 ISBN 0-02-018870-6

Coover, Robert. *A Night at the Movies.*
$7.95 ISBN 0-02-019120-0

Dickinson, Charles. *With or Without.*
$7.95 ISBN 0-02-019560-5

Handke, Peter. *Across.*
$6.95 ISBN 0-02-051540-5

Handke, Peter. *Slow Homecoming.*
$8.95 ISBN 0-02-051530-8

Hemingway, Ernest. *The Garden of Eden.*
$8.95 ISBN 0-684-18871-6

Olson, Toby. *The Woman Who Escaped from Shame.*
$7.95 ISBN 0-02-023231-4

Pelletier, Cathie. *The Funeral Makers.*
$6.95 ISBN 0-02-023610-7

Phillips, Caryl. *A State of Independence.*
$6.95 ISBN 0-02-015080-6

Rush, Norman. *Whites.*
$6.95 ISBN 0-02-023841-X

Vargas Llosa, Mario. *Who Killed Palomino Molero?*
$6.95 ISBN 0-02-022570-9

West, Paul. *Rat Man of Paris.*
$6.95 ISBN 0-02-026250-7

*Available at your local bookstore, or from
Macmillan Publishing Company, 100K Brown Street
Riverside, New Jersey 08370*